VIGILANTE JUSTICE

VIGILANTE JUSTICE

PRESTON LEWIS

WHEELER PUBLISHING
A part of Gale, a Cengage Company

GALE
A Cengage Company

Wheeler Publishing Large Print Softcover Western.
The text of this Large Print edition is unabridged.
Other aspects of the book may vary from the original edition.
Set in 16 pt. Plantin.

LIBRARY OF CONGRESS CIP DATA ON FILE.
CATALOGUING IN PUBLICATION FOR THIS BOOK
IS AVAILABLE FROM THE LIBRARY OF CONGRESS.

ISBN-13: 978-1-4328-9327-9 (softcover alk. paper)

Published in 2022 by arrangement with Preston Lewis

Printed in the United States of America
1 2 3 4 5   26 25 24 23 22

For Greg Tobin,
both a friend and
the editor who let me in on a Bonanza

1

The pale yellow light of the kerosene lamp was suddenly overwhelmed by a blinding white flash that lit the kitchen brighter than day. Instantly, the nearby lightning bolt exploded in a booming peal of thunder. The thunderclap rumbled like a stampede over Hugh Hampton's two-room cabin, rattling the windowpanes to his side and the wooden plank floor at his feet.

Startled by the sudden explosion of the sky, Hampton dropped his spoon into the tin of beans that was his meager supper. Beneath the plank table where he sat, his frightened cur Andy shivered against his boots.

Instinctively, Hampton lifted the burlap curtain he had cut from a potato sack and glanced outside. As dry as things had been, the lightning could easily start a fire. As bad as this spring had been, Hampton half expected to find his barn ablaze, but he saw no flame or embers anywhere, just another flash of lightning. The crack of thunder drew a whine from Andy.

The thunderstorm was just more bad luck. Hampton could accept the lightning and thunder, provided the cloud released some of its moisture for the parched earth. Instead the cloud merely threatened the land and mocked its thirst. Hampton knew the spring grass lay yellow and limp. Hampton knew Pecan Creek beyond his barn was but a trickle, its meager water pooling stagnant and green in places. Hampton knew that a man's sweat and blood could make a place but never irrigate it. Brown County and all of West Texas needed rain.

In the next flash of lightning, Hampton saw the scattered live oak and mesquite that had staked their own claim on his ranch land. Beyond the barn, Hampton saw the ribbon of pecan trees that lined the creek and gave it its name. Just as quickly as the world had been lit, it went dark again. But in that final instant of white light, Hampton caught his breath.

Something was out there!

Hampton didn't believe in ghosts, yet if he could believe his eyes, that was just what he had seen.

At his feet, Andy suddenly quit cowering

and began to growl. The dog darted from under the table to the door and planted his feet to attack. Andy would never let anyone within a hundred yards of the cabin without setting up a commotion that would scare any sane man away.

As looks went, Andy wasn't much of a dog. By the way he carried his tail and his reddish-gray coloring, with rusty highlights around the legs, feet and ears, Hampton figured Andy was part coyote, his height, length and forty-five-pound weight very similar to a full-grown coyote's build. Andy's head appeared lopsided because his left ear had been gnawed off in some previous encounter. Another scar, a fifteen-inch strip of pink flesh along the left withers, peeked out from behind his mangy fur. Andy feared nothing but thunder.

In another quick flash of lightning, Hampton saw the specter again. Tall as a man astride a horse, the shapeless mass seemed to quiver in the wind. It had to be a ghost; nothing else but a fool would venture out in a thunderstorm like this. Through the rush of the wind and the rustle of the trees, Hampton heard an eerie, moaning sound.

"Oooooooh, oooooooh," came the noise, raising the hackles on the back of Andy's neck.

Hampton released the burlap curtain and shoved his lean, five-eleven, hundred-and-seventy pound frame away from the table. He lunged for the Henry carbine by the door. As he levered a cartridge into the chamber, he could feel sweat beading in his sandy-brown hair and mustache. Fear had been an infrequent companion in his life. This fear was foolish, he knew, but he was driven by a dread of something sinister. Maybe it was the thunderstorm itself, or perhaps the drought.

Or, maybe it was Lemuel Blunt!

Blunt ran the Lazy B, the biggest ranch in Brown County, but he had been stretched to the breaking point by the drought and had taken to threatening the smaller neighboring ranches, especially those along Pecan Creek on land he had once claimed. The law, though, had invalidated most of his claim, and Blunt had lost to men like Hugh Hampton more than three-quarters of the creek front he had once used to water his cattle. The loss hadn't mattered in the good years, but now that water was scarce, Blunt's cattle were dying.

Not that anyone sympathized with Blunt, considering the way he treated his two grown daughters. Rumor had it that he regularly sold them out to his ranch hands.

The worst Hell's Half Acre madam in Fort Worth treated her girls better than Blunt did his own flesh and blood, said many Brown County residents — though never within hearing range of Blunt, who many believed had killed his Comanche wife six years ago. Under the right circumstances, Blunt could be a threat to any man, woman or child in Brown County.

Then again, maybe this ghost was just Hampton's imagination. He would find out. Gently, Hampton lifted the latch and released the handle so the wind pushed the door open. Andy dodged the door, then lunged out onto the porch, barking and growling. Hampton stepped out behind him and lifted his carbine to his shoulder.

Lightning flashed and the ghost took on a yellow hue. The specter drew nearer, close enough that Hampton could make out its amorphous shape, even in the darkness. It made a strange noise that reminded Hampton of a tent flap flopping in the wind.

Andy advanced to the edge of the porch, growling.

The ghost moaned again. *"Oooooooh, oooooooh."*

Suddenly, Andy quit growling, then barked once and turned around, moving leisurely toward the door.

Hampton glanced from the ghost to Andy, lowering his gun as he turned back to the ghost. "Who is it?"

"Oooooooh Huuuugh," answered the ghost.

Hampton lowered his carbine. The voice now had a vague familiarity. "What the hell?"

The ghost came closer yet, then stopped not two strides from Hampton's cabin. "They're dead," called the ghost, "both of them."

In the dim but constant light that seeped out of the cabin, Hampton could make out a canvas slicker draped over the head of a horse, and then a hatless rider with another canvas slicker drawn up over his head. "Who's dead?"

"Both of them, dammit."

Then Hampton recognized the voice. It belonged to Let Gibson. "Is that you, Let?"

"Who the hell you think it was?"

Lightning lit the sky again and Hampton saw up close how foolish his neighbor looked. "You've been drinking again, haven't you, Let? Nothing but a drunk or a fool would be out riding with it storming like this." Hampton twisted around and leaned his Henry back inside the cabin.

"Yes, sir, I've been drinking, but I ain't no Baptist so I figger I can take a snort or two after what I seen."

Hampton stepped off the porch and gently pulled the canvas slicker from the horse, so as not to spook it. Then he took the reins and tied them to a post supporting the porch overhang.

"You see any rain, Let?"

"Hell, no, dammit. And I can cuss, too, not being no Baptist."

"Then why the slickers over you and your horse?" Hampton asked as he stepped to Gibson's side to pull him from his mount.

"Why you fool, I was hiding from the lightning. Don't want to get killed."

Hampton shook his head. Gibson was drunker than he had thought. Hampton grabbed Gibson's arm just as a bolt of lightning crashed to the earth not a hundred yards back down the road.

Gibson panicked. He jerked his arm from Hampton's grasp and jumped off the opposite side of the horse, but his boot caught for an instant in his stirrup and he slammed to the ground. Instantly, he came up, his arms windmilling. "They're gonna blow us all up, like they did the Gillyard brothers."

Hampton dashed around the fidgeting mount, grabbed Gibson by the arm and jerked him up onto the porch and into his cabin. "What about the Gillyard brothers?"

13

Gibson shielded his eyes from the lamplight as Hampton helped him inside. "They blew up their place, killed them both."

"Who's they?" Hampton asked.

"The Gillyard brothers, dammit."

Shaking his head, Hampton steered Gibson to a chair at his table, then backtracked to the door, which he latched as Andy retreated under the table. "How long you been drinking, Let?"

Gibson fumbled to pull his slicker off, but got tangled in it until Hampton freed his arms. "I been drinking since I found where my pappy stowed his liquor."

Hampton let out a slow breath of disgust. "Today, Let, when did you start drinking today?"

"About noontime, when the heat kicked in."

"And what were you doing out in this kind of weather?"

"Matilda kicked me out until I sobered up, so I went over to see the Gillyard brothers and share a drink with them. They don't mind a fellow taking a drink. But the place blowed up before I got there. I seen it."

Hampton shook his head. "You sure it wasn't just lightning you saw?"

Gibson cocked his head in exasperation. "I know what I seen and their place was

14

blowed up."

"You're drunk."

Gibson folded his arms across his chest and nodded. "I'll be sober come morning but their place'll still be blowed up."

Hampton considered brewing a pot of coffee to help sober up Gibson, but decided against it because the kitchen was hot enough without building another fire, and a ton of coffee probably wouldn't sober Gibson up any quicker than a night's sleep. Instead, Hampton picked up his plate of cold beans from beside Gibson and slid it under the table, where Andy still shivered with every thunderclap from the retreating storm. Andy quickly lapped up the beans. Nice thing about the dog was it didn't complain about Hampton's cooking. And it didn't get drunk.

When sober, Let Gibson was a shrewd rancher and a good judge of horseflesh. When drunk, he was a poor judge of anything. Gibson, at least sixty years old, and his younger wife ran a small ranch, also on Pecan Creek, about six miles northwest of Hampton's place. The Gillyard place, a modest farm of a hundred and sixty acres on Pecan Creek, was wedged between the two ranches. A small man, Gibson stood five feet four inches tall in boots and tipped the scales at no more than a hundred and thirty-five pounds. Though small, he had deceptive strength, made more dangerous by his temper, which was as fiery as his red hair and his ruddy complexion. Much to the amusement of other ranchers, he wore overalls with a gun belt strapped outside. Hampton noted that Gibson's battered straw hat was missing, likely knocked or blown off during his ride through the storm.

Come morning, Hampton would escort Gibson as far as the Gillyard place to check on the two respected brothers. Along the way, Hampton would help Gibson find his hat. If he had believed Gibson's wild tale, Hampton would have saddled up and checked on the two farmers as soon as the storm passed.

Gradually, Gibson began to slump forward in his chair, the weight of all the liquor dragging him toward sleep. "They blowed up the Gillyard brothers," he mumbled.

Hampton stepped to Gibson and shook his shoulder. "Who blew up the Gillyard brothers?"

Gibson tried to lift his sagging head to see who was talking, but he just collapsed on the table, out cold. Hampton left him where he was, his head and chest resting on the table where Hampton normally played a game or two of solitaire with his dog-eared deck of cards. Hampton's other diversion from ranch work was a subscription to *Leslie's Weekly,* but the lamp was burning low and he doubted he could concentrate, not with Gibson's loud snoring.

Outside, the storm's passing was marked only by occasional flashes in the distant sky and the low grumble of thunder. Andy emerged from under the table and pawed at the door to let Hampton know he was ready to go outside for the night. Hampton obliged the dog, then stood on the porch watching the large cloud to the east light up with its own fire. He untied Gibson's black stallion and led him to the barn, where he put the animal up for the night in the pen with his own gelding.

As Hampton returned to his cabin, Andy prowled the perimeter of the barn, back to his old inquisitive self now that the storm had passed. Hampton latched the door, then grabbed the Henry carbine and retreated into his small bedroom. He undressed quickly and went to bed, sleep coming slowly because of Gibson's loud snoring and his own fears that perhaps something more than the storm and the drunk Gibson had passed over the Gillyard place.

Come sunrise, Hampton plied Gibson

with a half-dozen cups of coffee and had two cups for himself, his only breakfast. Gibson said little, groaning occasionally and constantly pinching at the bridge of his nose.

After saddling the horses and leading them to the house, Hampton got his carbine and led Gibson outside to his stallion. Gibson rejected Hampton's attempt to help him mount. He wobbled as he climbed into the saddle, then reached to tug his missing hat down over his head. He cursed and turned back down the road.

Hampton shoved his carbine in his saddle scabbard, mounted quickly, then started after Gibson. They rode without a word for two miles, until Hampton spotted Gibson's straw hat on the trail. He dismounted and picked it up, dusting it against his britches before offering it to Gibson. The rancher jerked it from Hampton's hand and tugged it into place, then nudged his horse into a trot.

Hampton scurried to mount and catch up. They rode side by side for the final mile to the Gillyard farm. When the trail curved around the last grove of live oaks, Hampton got a full view of the Gillyard place — or what was left of it.

Drunk or not, Gibson had been right.

2

Let Gibson lifted his arm and pointed at the rubble. "I may've been drunk, but I was damn sure right, Hugh."

Hampton slumped in his saddle and shook his head. What had been the Gillyards' meager cabin was little more than kindling, its walls splintered, the lumber broken like matchsticks, and its roof missing, the wooden shingles scattered for fifty yards around the place.

"You figger it was Blunt's men that did this?"

Hampton left the question hanging as he nudged his gelding into a trot and approached the debris. The powerful explosion had scattered clothes, utensils and furniture in all directions. A workshirt clung to a hitching post; a rocking chair hung from the limb of a mesquite tree that shaded the southern side of the cabin; and a fork was impaled in a table sheared of all but one leg.

Beyond the shattered cabin, the sturdy shed that served as a small barn still stood, but its walls were embedded with wooden shrapnel from the explosion. The Gillyard brothers' milch cow, plow oxen and three horses were dead in the corral beside the shed.

Hampton pointed to what was left of the small earthen dam the Gillyards had engineered to hold water when the creek ran full. No one had complained when the Gillyards built the dam, and when the creek ran low, the Gillyard brothers had allowed Hampton, Gibson and the other small ranchers to water their stock there until it dried up. Only Lemuel Blunt had not been invited to water his stock. "They blew up the dam," Hampton said.

Gibson nodded. "I figger it was Blunt."

"We need proof." Hampton dismounted, holding the reins of his chestnut and leading the gelding through the litter. He stopped and toed at a book splayed and crumpled upon the ground. It was a Bible. Many times he had seen the Gillyard brothers sitting on the porch and reading the Good Book after a long day's work. Industrious and honest, the Gillyards had been decent men, respected by most who made Brown County home.

Squatting beside the Bible, Hampton picked it up by the spine and shut it carefully, noting the splotches of blood on its pages. One of the Gillyards likely was reading it when the explosion occurred. Standing up slowly, Hampton eased over to his gelding and placed the Bible in his saddlebag.

As he looked over the rump of his gelding, he saw what he'd hoped he would not find. Crumpled against a section of displaced wall reposed a fleshy pulp that had once been one of the Gillyards. Hampton pointed. "There's one of them."

"Or what's left of him." Gibson shook his head.

Hampton angled toward the corpse, leading his gelding and picking up a blanket that had snagged upon a wall plank. His chestnut tossed his head and jerked at the reins, protesting Hampton's approach to the corpse. Hampton released the gelding's leather straps and stared at the body, sickened by what explosives could do to a living, breathing man. He shook his head as he draped the blanket over the remains. "We need to find the other one."

Gibson rode his black stallion to Hampton's horse and grabbed its reins. He maneuvered both horses to a nearby mesquite tree and dismounted, tying their reins to a low limb. "Damn shame, Hugh. These were fine old boys."

Hampton wandered among the debris, looking for the second body. Disgust rose like bile in him. Was Lemuel Blunt so despicable as to do this type of thing? Hampton knew the answer and knew that he, too, was in danger unless Blunt was brought to justice. Gradually, Hampton worked his way out to the corral and shed without seeing sign of the second body. Behind the shed, he found a length of discarded fuse. As he bent to pick up the four inches of jute fuse, he spotted a trail of scorched earth snaking toward the demolished cabin.

"Over here," yelled Gibson, waving his straw hat at Hampton. "I found the other one." He pointed to the base of a cistern at the corner of the house. Never ones to waste anything, the Gillyard brothers had rigged up gutters on each side of the house to drain rainwater into the cistern.

His stomach churning, Hampton stood up, shoved the fuse in his pocket and headed for the cabin ruins. As he approached Gibson and the body, Hampton was revolted at the bloody form. A table leg was impaled through the man's chest and his bloodied face was flattened featureless. Hampton sighed and turned quickly away. "Let's find something to cover him up."

Gibson stepped over what was left of a cabin wall and stirred among the jumble created by the explosion. "Here's some canvas," he yelled, bending and pulling a tarpaulin from beneath the clutter. One end of the canvas was shredded and ripped, the tatters snagging in the debris until Gibson cursed and used his deceptive strength to jerk it free. He dragged it to Hampton.

Taking a deep breath, Hampton considered pulling the table leg from the man's chest, but decided it best to leave it as was for the sheriff to see. Hampton grabbed an end of the canvas and gritted his teeth as he began to drape it over the body. Both bodies were so badly mutilated, Hampton knew no one would be able to tell one brother from the other.

Gibson grimaced, then turned quickly away from the body. "Damn the bastards that did this."

Hampton spat at a broken chair. "They lit the fuse out behind the shed." He pulled the length of jute fuse from his pocket and shook it at Gibson.

Shoving his hands in the back pockets of his overalls, Gibson turned toward the shed and Pecan Creek behind it. "I figger they hid their horses among the trees on the other side of the creek."

Hampton stared beyond the trees toward the Lazy B and nodded. "Lem Blunt's side of the creek." Hampton strode to the back side of the cabin, spotting the fuse's powder burn at the base of what had once been a wall. From there, he followed the burn marks back to the shed, Gibson tailing him the entire way. At the end of the scorch marks, Hampton began to move in arcs away from the shed, looking for the tracks of the murderer. The ground was so dry that he found nothing definitive until he reached the creek bed, where the trickle of water left enough moisture in its trail to soften the ground.

Gibson spotted them first. "There," he called, pointing off to Hampton's right.

Following the direction of Gibson's finger, Hampton saw the tracks. He eased that direction, grabbing Gibson's arm to keep him from tramping over the boot prints, which retreated from the Gillyard cabin. Carefully, he studied them. "Three, maybe four men," he said. Beyond those tracks, he observed another set, this group aimed

24

straight for the house.

Gibson's gaze was just a moment behind Hampton's. "There's where they crossed over to begin with, I figger."

Hampton stroked his chin. "Bring up the horses, Let, and stay clear of the tracks here. Before we fetch the sheriff, we'll see if we can pick up the trail."

"Be right back," Let answered, darting off toward the mesquite tree where the horses were hitched.

Hampton jumped over the mushy middle of the creek and lined up the murderers' retreating tracks with the shed, then started across the yellowed grass for the grove of live oaks fifty yards away. Though the ground was hard, Hampton was able to follow the trail of trampled grass.

Behind him he heard Gibson approaching on horseback. Hampton turned and waved Gibson away. "Make a wide circle so we don't disturb their tracks."

Gibson aimed the horses clear of the trail Hampton followed to the grove of live oaks. On the back side of the grove, he found trampled grass and fresh horse droppings that had not yet crusted over. He toed at the manure, shaking his head in anger. As he looked over the area, a splotch of white by one of the live oaks caught his eye. He bent over and picked up a muslin sack with the familiar label of Blackwell's genuine Bull Durham smoking tobacco. A lot of men in Brown County smoked Bull Durham, Lemuel Blunt among them. Hampton shoved the empty tobacco sack in his pocket with the length of fuse, then angled toward Gibson, who had stopped the horses a dozen paces from Hampton.

"Found a Durham tobacco sack."

"Isn't that what Blunt smokes?" Gibson handed Hampton his reins.

"That's my recollection," Hampton said as he mounted his gelding. "We can go to the sheriff first or follow the trail."

Gibson nodded. "We both know where it leads."

"All the more reason to follow it, Let, so there's absolutely no doubt." Hampton turned his gelding toward the Blunt place, reminding Gibson once again to stay wide of the trail so it would be unsullied when they returned with the sheriff.

The tracks were easy to follow because the horses' shoes cut into the hard ground and made a greater impression upon the earth than the footstep of a booted man. The trail was as straight and true as Hampton had expected, leading from the Gillyard place onto the Lazy B ranch. It was five miles from the Gillyard cabin to Blunt's modest ranch house, and the trail Hampton paralleled never varied its aim.

Hampton and Gibson advanced wordlessly until they neared a tree-rimmed rise that spread out into a narrow valley. They reined up their mounts and dismounted, tying the horses to trees, then advancing afoot to a clump of rocks at the base of the rise. From there they could see the Blunt ranch house. Instinctively, both men let their hands fall to their guns. With his right hand, Hampton reached across his waist and pulled the butt-reversed Colt .45 from the holster on his left hip.

"You should've gotten your Henry from your horse," Gibson whispered as they slipped among the rocks. "You're the best damn long shot in Brown County."

"I didn't come to kill them," Hampton answered.

"Before this is over, you may wish you had."

As he maneuvered between the rocks, Hampton's boot slipped and he heard the clink of glass. He stopped and looked at his foot, wedged between two stones. There he saw a couple whiskey bottles, one full, the other half-empty.

Seeing his discovery, Gibson bent to

inspect them. "This is good liquor."

"No drinking now, Let," Hampton shot back. "We'll look the place over from here, then head into town for the sheriff."

Gibson sighed with regret. "This is expensive liquor. Must be one of Blunt's men doesn't want to share this with the rest."

"Either that," Hampton laughed, "or one of his daughters doesn't want to share it with her old man."

Gibson scratched his head. "Those girls might be damn pretty if he hadn't raised them like boys. They dress in shirt and pants, ride like men and I even heard one of them cuss enough to embarrass the devil."

Hampton shook his head. "Even in pants they ain't bad looking. Hell, Let, I don't have Matilda to go home to every night."

"That can be arranged," Gibson answered, "if you'll trade that damn dog for her." Gibson laughed.

Taking off his hat, Hampton lifted his head over a rock and studied the Blunt ranch house a quarter-mile away. Though nothing fancy, the house was more than adequate. Except for the ribbon of smoke coming out of the stovepipe and the horses in the corral, the place was still.

"The trail leads where we knew it would,"

Gibson offered.

"Yep, and now's time for us to fetch the sheriff."

"You figger he'll do anything? He's a mite friendly with Blunt."

"How can he not do something?" Hampton asked.

"By sitting on his lazy butt, that's how."

The two men lowered their heads and backtracked through the rocks, Gibson lingering beside the two whiskey bottles. "I'm a touch thirsty, Hugh. I figger I could take one of these bottles along to keep me company."

Hampton grabbed Gibson's arm and pulled him toward the horses. "Hell, Let, it's not even nine o'clock and you're already thinking about drinking. Besides, we don't want anyone to know we were here."

Gibson shook his head. "Damn shame to leave good whiskey all alone out here, Hugh."

The two men untied their horses and aimed them toward Brownwood and the sheriff's office, ten miles away. They rode at an easy pace and made it into town well before noon, heading straight for the sheriff's office.

The jail was a simple stone structure that several in county government suggested should be replaced by a grand two- or three-story building that the town and county could be proud of. Hampton didn't see much sense in constructing such a fine building to be occupied by some of the county's worst citizens, but many good folks in West Texas invested a lot of civic pride in their jail, and Hampton knew a grand edifice would eventually be built.

Hampton and Gibson dismounted outside the jail. They strode up to the door, which flew open just as Hampton was about to grab the handle.

Sheriff Perry Johns stood, hat in hand, in the doorway. He was tall and as lean as forty years of drought. He greeted Hampton with a hacking cough and an impatient wave of his hand, which was fixed around a smoldering cigarette.

"There's been a murder, Sheriff," Gibson started out.

"That a fact, Let, or have you been drinking and imagining things?"

"It's true," Hampton answered. "The Gillyard brothers are dead, their house blown up."

The sheriff backtracked and motioned for the two to enter. "You don't say."

"And we know who did it," Gibson interjected again.

Hampton wished Gibson would quit volunteering so much information.

"That a fact?" the sheriff said.

"Yeah," Gibson answered. "Lemuel Blunt and his men."

So fast did he cast his stare at Gibson, Johns almost spun his head out of its socket. "That a fact?"

Gibson nodded, but the sheriff turned to Hampton.

"That a fact, Hugh?"

Still uncertain of the lay of the land in the sheriff's mind, Hampton weighed how to respond before answering. "We followed tracks of the murderers from the Gillyard place to Blunt's ranch."

Johns stroked his whisker-stubbled chin. "That's a serious accusation to make against the biggest rancher in all of Brown County."

"Reporting what I've seen."

Johns nodded. "That's not important, Hugh. What's important is what I see."

"Then perhaps you best come along with us and let us show you what we know," Hampton shot back.

3

As they emerged from the grove of live oaks into full view of the demolished Gillyard cabin, Hugh Hampton jerked his carbine from the saddle boot and leveled it at his shoulder. Before Let Gibson or the sheriff could react, Hampton squeezed off two quick shots. Two coyotes sniffing at one of the Gillyard corpses dropped dead and a third scampered away. A half-dozen others looked up from the livestock carrion they were devouring in the corral, then scattered when Hampton fired two more shots. One retreating coyote yelped, then limped on three legs for cover.

"Damnation," said Gibson, "you're faster with that Henry than most men are with their revolvers."

Hampton lowered his carbine, its barrel trailing smoke as he ejected an empty hull. He pulled four cartridges from his gun belt and replenished his rifle.

Sheriff Perry Johns was impressed with neither Hampton's deadly aim nor the remains of the Gillyard brothers' cabin. He paused and pulled a bag of tobacco from his vest pocket and slowly built himself a smoke.

Hampton slid his Henry back in its saddle boot as the sheriff flicked a match to life with his thumbnail. The match flared, then flamed at the twist of paper at the end of the cigarette. The sheriff sucked the flame into the tobacco until the cigarette glowed at the tip. The sheriff flicked the lit match to the ground.

Instantly, Hampton jumped from his saddle and stomped out the match in a clump of dry grass, admonishing the sheriff for his carelessness. "As dry as it's been, you best be more careful, before you burn up all of Brown County."

"The drought's made you awfully jumpy, Hugh." The sheriff shrugged as he sucked on his cigarette.

"The dynamiting of my friends' place — that's made me jumpy." Hampton pulled himself back in the saddle, then pointed at the cabin remains. "Now do you believe me?"

The sheriff exhaled a ribbon of smoke as he shrugged again. "The place is destroyed.

I can see that. But dynamited? I don't know that I've seen anything that would prove that."

Hampton felt his anger building with his frustration. "How else could you explain it?"

"Bad cloud came through last night, Hugh. Could've been a damn cyclone."

"Cyclone?" Hampton spoke with disgust. "You haven't even seen the place up close."

The sheriff shook his head. "That's right. I've been here jabbering with you."

With his knee, Hampton nudged his horse forward. Gibson's stallion quickly came abreast of him. Gibson leaned over and whispered, "I told you the sheriff was in cahoots with Blunt."

"What was that you said?" the sheriff demanded of Let.

"I said you was a buddy to old man Blunt."

The sheriff pulled his cigarette from his lips and pointed it at Gibson. "I'm a friend of all law-abiding citizens of Brown County. And right now, I ain't see anything that proves your allegation."

Gibson flared with anger. "It's because you ain't been looking, Sheriff."

"I've been looking, Let. It's just that I ain't been seeing exactly the same thing you're seeing. Until I've got proof, all I've got is your guesswork."

Gibson scoffed, "At least I'm working at it; that's more than I can say . . ."

Hampton grabbed Gibson's arm. "Ease off, Let. Don't anger him so that he'll ignore the obvious."

At the edge of the circle of debris, Hampton dismounted and aimed toward the nearest body. Gibson followed Hampton's lead, but the sheriff stayed atop his sorrel, which moved with less restraint through the wreckage.

Reaching the first body, Hampton shook his head. The coyotes had pulled the blanket off the corpse and begun to gnaw on his leg. In frustration, Hampton kicked the two dead coyotes.

The sheriff reined up his horse and shook his head. "Yep, he's dead all right, but I ain't seen nothing that says dynamite's what did it. I still figure a damn cyclone came through and demolished the cabin."

Hampton shrugged and let out a deep breath of exasperation. He angled for the cistern in disgust. Gibson was right. The sheriff would defend Lemuel Blunt against any accusation. At the base of the cistern, he bent and lifted the tarp from the second victim of the bombing. "Here's the other one."

Flicking his spent cigarette aside, Sheriff Johns eased his sorrel that direction.

Hampton saw Gibson angle toward the smoldering remnants of the smoke and crush it with his boot. Hampton could only shake his head again. In disgust, he dropped the reins of his chestnut. "The Gillyards were good men, Sheriff. They didn't deserve to die like this."

The sheriff stopped his sorrel beside the cistern, then leaned forward, resting his hands on the saddle horn. "I still ain't seen nothing that shows me they was blowed up. Still could've been a cyclone, Hugh."

Jerking the tarp back over the second body, Hugh spun around and planted both fists on his hips. "If there was a tornado, why didn't it leave a trail of destruction beyond the cabin?"

"I've seen cyclones dangle from the sky like a twirling lariat, bouncing across the landscape. Until you show me some proof, I ain't changing my mind."

Hampton strode to what remained of the back wall. "Then look at this, dammit."

The sheriff grinned at Hampton's anger. Straightening in the saddle, Johns moved toward Hampton.

Straddling the burnt trail of the fuse, Hampton pointed to the hole at the base of the cabin and the blast marks upon what remained of the cabin walls. "There's your evidence, Sheriff."

Johns eased his sorrel behind Hampton, stopping atop the fuse's scorch marks. The horse danced nervously, lifting and dropping its feet upon the trail of the fuse.

At first Hampton thought the horse was just a nervous type, but then he saw the slight flick of the sheriff's wrist and tightening of his knee against the horse. Hampton then realized the sheriff was trying to obliterate the burn marks on the ground.

The sheriff took off his hat and squinted at the evidence. As he replaced his hat, he nodded. "Looks like there was a little explosion. So what, it doesn't look big enough to have destroyed the cabin. Anyway, most folks knew the Gillyards used dynamite now and then to blast stumps in their fields. The fellow by the cistern could've set off a stick or two by accident."

Hampton felt his jaw drop. He could not believe the sheriff was ignoring the obvious, that the Gillyard brothers had been murdered.

"That hole and the burn marks on the wall could've been caused by a lightning strike. You know what a bad storm that was last night. A cyclone's still my guess. That and lightning."

Hampton spat, then pointed at the fuse trail. "How would lightning create the fuse trail you've been trying to erase?"

Johns played dumb, offering Hampton a shrug and a sly grin. "What are you talking about?"

Hampton strode by him, pointing at the scorch marks.

The sheriff twisted around in his saddle to watch Hampton, then turned his sorrel about.

"There, now explain the fuse burns on the ground. A man that blew up his cabin by accident damn sure wouldn't lay a fuse trail."

"Hell, Hugh, for all you know the Gillyards could've had a spat and things could've gotten out of hand, one trying to get the other."

In exasperation, Hampton turned from the sheriff and made straight for the small barn. As he strode, he pulled from his britches pocket the fuse remnant he had found. Glancing back over his shoulder, he saw the sheriff still sitting on his horse and watching. "You coming or not?" Hampton challenged.

The sheriff rattled the reins and his sorrel followed Hampton to the barn.

Hampton turned his head from the sheriff and followed the snaking trail of the fuse burn. As he marched, he shook the fuse remnant and spoke, his voice rising in frustration. "I found this behind the barn, part of the fuse someone lit, in case you care."

Johns laughed. "All I care about is getting at the truth."

Hampton scoffed. "You sure aren't putting much stock in what I've found."

"In my line of work, Hugh, you don't accept the obvious. For all I know, you could've done this."

His anger on the verge of exploding, Hampton clenched his teeth as he reached the small barn. Damn the sheriff.

Johns rode around the shed, appearing bored with Hampton's explanation.

"Here's where the fuse was lit."

"So? How's that tie in with Lem Blunt, Hugh?" The sheriff's face had reddened in anger. "You and Let came to town, accusing Lem Blunt and his boys of doing this. Where's the proof?"

Hampton flung the strand of fuse to the ground and shoved his hand back in his pocket, extracting the Bull Durham pouch.

He shook the pouch at chin level. "I found this behind the thicket of live oaks across the creek. I figure it's Blunt's."

The sheriff laughed. "Is that a fact? It's been a few years since I checked, but I don't remember Lem being the only man to use Bull Durham in Brown County." With a taunting smile upon his lips, the sheriff dipped his fingers into his vest pocket and pulled out his own bag of Bull Durham. He shook it at Hampton. "I suspect this means I was involved in the bombing or the accident or the cyclone or whatever the hell it was that killed the Gillyards."

Shoving the pouch back in his pocket, Hampton grimaced. "We found tracks, followed them from the live oaks all the way to Lem Blunt's place." Starting for the creek and its trickle of water, Hampton pointed to the dam. "They blew up the dam, too. You and I both know Lem Blunt had threatened the Gillyards for not letting him water any stock there."

Receiving no response, Hampton glanced back over his shoulder to see the sheriff sitting on his motionless horse.

"You coming or not?"

Johns touched the heel of his boot to the animal's flank and the sorrel started ahead.

At the creek, Hampton pointed out the

two places where the assassins had crossed. Johns rode over to inspect both sites, each time trampling the tracks with the hooves of his horse until the original tracks were obliterated. The sheriff pointed to a single set of tracks a ways back up the creek. "Whose are those?"

"Mine," Hampton admitted.

"Who's to say you weren't involved in the killings, Hugh? How'd you find out about the explosion?"

"Last night Let rode over drunk, talking about it. I just figured it was the liquor talking, no truth to it."

The sheriff cackled with a mocking laugh. "Who's to say Let didn't do it?"

"I am!"

Hampton turned to see Let standing behind the sheriff's sorrel, holding the reins for his black stallion and Hampton's chestnut gelding. Johns twisted in his saddle, glaring at Gibson.

"I didn't have nothing to do with it, except finding it," Gibson stated.

Shrugging, Johns began to work on the makings of another cigarette, occasionally nodding to himself and looking down at Hampton and Gibson. After spreading tobacco on a paper, he licked the paper edge and rolled it over the brown weed until he had a soggy, brown cigarette. He shoved the cigarette in his mouth and its makings back in his vest pocket, pulling out a match which he flicked against the end of his thumb. A flame balled at the match tip as he held it to his cigarette and inhaled deeply. The sheriff shook the flame to death, then flicked the dead match at Hampton. "There, in case you want to see if that match is out."

Hampton swatted the matchstick to the ground, then started for the thicket of live oak trees. Gibson led his stallion and Hampton's chestnut across the creek bed before the sheriff nudged his sorrel into an easy walk.

When Hampton reached the far side of the thicket, he motioned for Let to wait on the outer perimeter so as not to obliterate the horse tracks they had observed earlier.

The sheriff, though, rode past Gibson and ignored Hampton's uplifted arms, signaling him to stop. "What's the point here, Hugh?"

"Nothing, Sheriff, if you keep riding across their tracks. This is where the assassins hid their horses. Best I can make out, there were four or five of them."

"That a fact?" the sheriff said halfheartedly.

"Their trail leads right to Lem Blunt's place."

The sheriff rode his horse a ways down the previous tracks, then circled wide and returned to the thicket. He pointed to a set of parallel tracks. "Whose are those?"

"Mine and Let's. We followed the other trail to the Blunt place."

Johns laughed. "Who's to say they didn't follow your tracks?"

"I am," Let Gibson shouted. "This is the most foolishness I've ever seen, Sheriff. Hugh's been showing you things that a blind man could see in the dark."

The sheriff drew deeply on his cigarette as he studied Gibson. "You best watch your mouth, Let. A fool like you can get in plenty trouble shooting off your mouth. There's a simple explanation for everything I've seen. Cyclone, lightning."

Hampton stepped between Gibson and the sheriff. "Then how do you explain the tracks leading away from here?"

"Can't say right now, but I figure to ask Lem Blunt next time I see him."

"What about today?" Hampton shot back. "Nothing's keeping you from riding over today. I'll even go with you."

"Me too," Let Gibson interjected.

The sheriff let out a sigh with a great cloud of tobacco smoke. "If that's what it takes, fellows, I guess that's what I'll do. If you want to come along, then mount up and we'll all just go find out for ourselves."

"Good deal," Gibson said, tossing the chestnut's reins to Hampton and shoving his foot in his stirrup.

Hampton grabbed him by the shoulder. "Hold on, Let. We can't both leave. Those coyotes'd be right back. And somebody needs to bury those boys."

Gibson shook his head. "I want to see Blunt's answer."

"I'm making the call on this one, Let."

"I can be of help."

"You can be of more help staying here and burying the Gillyards." Hampton stared hard at Sheriff Perry Johns when he spoke next. "And, if something happens to me, there'll be someone to say who I was last with."

4

When they topped the tree-rimmed rise overlooking the valley where Lemuel Blunt had made his home, Hugh Hampton reached across his waist for the holster riding on his left hip. He lifted the leather thong that held the gun in place during his ranch work.

Sheriff Perry Johns noted Hampton's preparation. "There'll be no gunplay, Hugh."

Those were the first words the sheriff had spoken since they had left Gibson behind to bury the Gillyards. The sheriff had been too busy riding directly atop the assassins' incriminating trail to talk. But what good was talking with a man who had already made up his mind, had already found a dozen other possible explanations for the Gillyards' brutal deaths? "I'll defend myself, if it comes to it."

"It won't come to it. There'll be no trouble."

Hampton shook his head. "I'm getting the feeling there'll be no justice, either."

The sheriff jerked his head around and stared at Hampton. "You've got a way of rubbing a man the wrong way, Hugh. I'd be real careful around Lem Blunt, if I were you."

Hampton glanced toward the Blunt place. Already, the old man himself had appeared out on the porch, and a couple of his men were angling from the bunkhouse toward their boss. Like most ranch houses in Brown County, the Blunt place had started out small. As prosperity came, rooms were added on, until the house was a strange amalgamation of log and mill-finished wood. Beyond the house was a bunkhouse, a toolshed and a large barn, the biggest in Brown County. Several corrals and pens abutted the barn. On his few visits to the Blunt place, Hampton had seen them filled with cattle and horses. Now they were empty. Beside the house, a modest garden, planted earlier in the spring, had wilted under the dry heat.

Lifting his hat, Hampton drew his sleeve across his forehead, then the corner of his eyes. The afternoon sun was scalding and

Hampton's forehead was pimpled with beads of salty sweat. If the perspiration got into his eyes, the sting of the salt might interfere with his vision. He knew he had to think clearly and see clearly when he approached the place. Replacing his hat, he bent forward to pat his chestnut on the neck. The horse was hot, his coat sticky with perspiration even though Hampton had not once pushed the horse beyond a walk on the ride to Blunt's front door. The horse needed water, but Hampton doubted he would be invited to quench the animal's thirst on Blunt property.

Nearing the house, Hampton saw Blunt's two daughters emerge onto the porch beside their father. They both wore jeans, boots, men's workshirts and hats hanging by chin cords around their necks. Though the young women had a hard edge to them from being raised as boys and having names like Charlie and Josie, Hampton thought them both comely females who would enhance any man's arm. Part Comanche, they had a golden skin and black hair that hung long and free down their backs. Their high cheekbones and narrow noses highlighted their dark eyes, which were both inviting and brooding.

Of the two, Charlie was the older, rumored

to be about twenty-two, and the one Hampton favored. A couple years younger, Josie was no less pretty, but seemed more embittered by her fate in life. Rumor had it that after his wife's mysterious death, Lemuel Blunt had told his daughters not to plan on getting married or leaving home. There was plenty of women's work to do around the place, and they were going to do it or he would kill them. It had also been suggested that he used his daughters as common prostitutes to serve his ranch hands — and possibly even himself.

Lemuel Blunt, a double-barreled shotgun cradled across his arms, stepped off the porch and advanced toward the sheriff and Hampton. After him came his four cowboys, their hands dangerously close to the guns at their sides. The two Blunt women stepped to the edge of the porch but remained in the shade.

Old man Blunt was a cadaver of a man with thin, spindly legs and arms and a leathery face with sunken cheeks, which an unruly black beard could not conceal. His beard glistened with sweat, and his thin lips, barely visible beneath the beard, held the nub of a cigarette. His nervous eyes flitted from side to side as Hampton approached with the sheriff. For a man reputed to be the wealthiest in Brown County, the rancher was dressed poorer than his cowboys. He wore britches mended and patched innumerable times, a shirt with a collar half torn off and a floppy, sweat-stained felt hat. Blunt kicked at the ground with his battered right boot.

Hampton and the sheriff reined up in front of Lemuel Blunt.

Blunt spat the cigarette butt at the ground halfway between them. "You must be damn hard up for deputies, Sheriff, if you're riding with Hugh Hampton."

The sheriff laughed along with Blunt's four cowboys and Josie. "Hate to bother you, Lem, but I've a bit of bad news," the sheriff said. "The Gillyard brothers are dead."

Blunt jerked his hat from his head and held it over his heart. "You don't say. That's a damn shame, Sheriff. I hope they died of thirst, the way they dammed up the creek and kept some folks from getting the water they had coming." He slapped the hat back on his head. "I really do appreciate the notification, Sheriff, though me and my boys are too busy to attend their burial."

The cowboys laughed at Blunt's joke like the hired hands they were.

"Sheriff," continued Blunt, "that still

don't explain why you brought Hugh Hampton along. He's no better than those Gillyard brothers were, moving in on a man's water and claiming it."

The sheriff nodded. "You see, Lem, Hugh says the Gillyards were murdered."

Blunt blinked his eyelids. "If he knows; he must've done it, least that's how it would appear to me."

Hampton saw the cowhands and Josie laugh again, but Charlie seemed almost embarrassed by the confrontation. Hampton studied Blunt before speaking. "The Gillyard place was dynamited last night. Tracks from their place led to a live oak thicket where I found this." Hampton shoved his hand into his pocket and pulled out the empty tobacco pouch with the Bull Durham markings. "From the live oak thicket, I followed at least four sets of tracks to your place this morning. Did you leave this behind last night, Blunt?"

Anger flamed in Blunt's eyes and behind him the hilarity stopped among the cowhands. "Don't know nothing about the Gillyards' problems, and I don't give a damn, either." Blunt moved his gaze to the sheriff. "Is he your deputy or not?"

Johns shook his head. "Nope, Lem. He just came along for the ride. Something destroyed the Gillyard place, no doubt. Hugh thinks it was dynamite that you and your men set. Me, I figure it was a cyclone and lightning."

Blunt turned his scowl back at Hampton. "It was a bad cloud that moved through last night."

Shaking his head, Hampton spoke. "Not that bad. You or your men buried dynamite along the back wall and lit the fuse out behind their shed. You blew up their house, then demolished the dam."

Patting the barrel of his shotgun, Blunt spat. "How do you know so much without being involved?"

"Common sense," Hampton answered.

"Did you do it?" Blunt challenged.

"No!"

"Neither did I," Blunt answered, waving his arm for his men to step forward. "So we've got a standoff, Hampton." Blunt's men lined up, two on either side of him. He addressed each one. "Cyrus McCurdy, did you dynamite the Gillyard place?"

McCurdy, a lanky, brown-haired saddle tramp known more for his skill with a gun than any cowboying skill, stared at Hampton with mean, narrow eyes. "Hell, no."

"Olean Evans, what about you?"

Evans, his stringy yellow hair hanging like

cobwebs from beneath his hat, smirked and swaggered past Blunt, all the time staring at Hampton. "Ain't done a thing 'cept work for you, boss."

Blunt pointed at another hand. "Bibb Aultrong, what about you? You dynamited any cabins or dams lately?"

Shaking his head vigorously, the dim-witted Aultrong took his hat from his balding head and rolled the brim between his fingers. "I don't like loud noises, I don't."

Blunt laughed. "Yeah, Bibb's scared of the thunder. He was under a bed last night when the storm rolled through."

The other three hands, the sheriff and Josie joined in on the laughter.

Aultrong stepped forward to defend himself. "That's sorta right, but I sleep in the bottom bunk."

Aultrong's explanation drew more laughter from his bunkmates.

"And what about you, Ivey Yates?" asked Blunt to the last of his hands.

Yates was as unsuited for cowboying as the twin-holstered gun rig on his hips. "You know I didn't. You and I were up playing cards till almost midnight while I waited my turn with Charlie."

Out of the corner of his eye, Hampton saw Charlie drop her head in shame. He felt sorry for her.

Blunt turned triumphantly back to the sheriff. "Well, sir, Sheriff, that's five of us that say we didn't dynamite the Gillyard place to one of him. This being a democratic country, I figure we're right about this and he is wrong. If it wasn't him, then it must've been a cyclone and lightning like you said."

The cowhands laughed again.

Johns nodded and turned to Hampton. "You satisfied?"

"Not until the Gillyards' killers are brought to justice, but it's apparent you're satisfied."

Blunt patted his shotgun again and nodded confidently. "Sheriff, it looks like you've got an itch that Josie over there might be able to scratch for you, if you're interested."

Hampton watched the sheriff nod, then turn red in the cheeks. "I might stay for a little supper. Give my horse time to rest and maybe drink a little of your water."

"Josie'll water your horse for you and fix your supper later." Blunt gave the sheriff an exaggerated wink, drawing guffaws from the cowhands.

Hampton glanced to Josie and saw the shame etched upon her face and overflowing her eyes.

"Pa," Charlie said, "let me fetch a pail of

water for the other horse."

Blunt scowled. "Hell, no, Hampton's just about to leave."

"Don't take it out on the horse, Pa."

The sheriff dismounted, nodding at Blunt. "Why not? It's the neighborly thing to do. And, you are still neighbors."

Blunt laughed. "Sure, Charlie, go ahead and water his horse, but just don't you go fixing him any supper."

All the men laughed, except Hampton, who was embarrassed by Blunt's humiliation of his daughters.

Josie took the reins from the sheriff and led his sorrel around the side of the house. Charlie moved shyly toward Hampton's chestnut and slid her fingers under the bridle. Her touch was gentle, for the chestnut never flinched.

"You men go about your work," Blunt said. "Sheriff, you just go on inside in the shade. I'll have Josie sprinkle down a bed you can rest on before your supper."

As Blunt watched, Charlie led the horse around the side of the house to a cistern, where Josie had already drawn a pail of water for the sheriff's horse. The horse had barely finished drinking when Hampton heard Blunt's strident voice.

"Josie, let that damn horse drink on his

own and you get in there and sprinkle the bed, then take off your clothes for the sheriff."

Shaking her head, Josie walked by, a grimace across her face.

Embarrassed for her sister, Charlie turned to the cistern and dropped a pail on the end of the rope into the water. After it filled, she pulled it out, taking a dipper and extracting a good cup of the cool liquid for Hampton. He took the dipper from her hand and studied the curves of her face and her figure, which was all-woman in spite of the men's clothes.

He drank the water slowly, enjoying it as much as his view of Charlie. When he was done, he gave her the dipper. "Why do you stay?"

Her lips went taut and she glanced over her shoulder. "He would kill me, maybe Josie, too."

She dumped the pail of water into a wooden bucket for watering livestock, then put it on the ground in front of Hampton's chestnut. The horse drank the water greedily.

Hampton wanted to visit with Charlie, but he knew it was dangerous to linger. "Thank you," he said, once his horse had finished drinking.

She smiled meekly, then followed him back to the front of the house where Blunt stood. "Get inside, Charlie," he commanded and she obeyed. Blunt had manufactured himself another cigarette and his face was blurred by a cloud of smoke. He smirked at Hampton.

"Let me tell you something," Blunt began, his voice a menacing growl. "When the rains were good, it didn't matter, you squeezing in on my water on Pecan Creek. Now it does. You ought to leave before cyclones and lightning hit your place. You, Let Gibson, Frank Winfrey, Spud Davis and Johnny Walls had best give up your places."

Hampton shook his head. "Never. We got them fair and square and put too much work into them to cave in."

Blunt shook his head. "I figured you were a stubborn man. That's why I let the sheriff have my daughter, so we could talk straight. If I ever find you on my land again, I'll kill you."

Beyond Blunt he saw Charlie standing in the door, shaking her head.

"Same goes for any of your neighbors." Blunt laughed in a cloud of smoke. "Y'all won't be neighbors much longer unless you're all buried side by side."

"Maybe you can cow the law, Blunt, but

you can't cow me and the other small operators." Hampton tugged on the reins and spun his horse around, then spurred the animal and dashed back toward the rise and the clump of rocks where one of Blunt's men stashed his whiskey.

Quickly he was over the rise and out of sight. He slowed the horse to a steady trot and aimed the chestnut for the Gillyard place. When he arrived, Gibson had just started covering the graves.

As he wiped sweat from his face and hands, Gibson watched Hampton approach and dismount. "How'd it go?"

"The sheriff was as yellow there as he was here. And Blunt as much as threatened the same thing for the rest of us."

"What did the sheriff say about that?"

"The sheriff was otherwise occupied when he made the threat."

"Josie or Charlie?" Gibson asked.

Hampton ignored the comment. "We best get the word out. It's you, me, Frank Winfrey, Spud Davis and Johnny Walls he's after. We'll meet in town tomorrow afternoon, discuss matters with that new lawyer there, that fellow named Spencer Yantis."

5

Spencer Yantis stood as straight as a states-man's statue, his years as a captain in the artillery having given him a commanding bearing in the presence of other men. His desk was as orderly as his legal mind. He believed in justice, but the six-gun at his side insinuated that justice did not always come from the law. He brushed his hand through his thinning hair as he looked around his crowded office.

Hugh Hampton and the four neighboring ranchers threatened by Lemuel Blunt sat in a semicircle around Yantis's rolltop desk, which abutted the back wall beneath a painting of Abraham Lincoln.

Beside Hampton, Let Gibson tapped his foot impatiently on the hardwood floor, his right hand sliding in and out of the pocket where he carried a flask of whiskey. Beside Gibson sat Johnny Walls, a young rancher who had bought out the previous owner and bought into a passel of problems with Blunt. Unlike the other owners around, Walls saw the benefit of combining ranching and farming to grow feed for his livestock rather than just letting them graze. The result was he could run more cattle on fewer acres than any other rancher in the county. When he wasn't working, he could be found reading agricultural circulars from the land-grant college.

Beyond Walls sat Frank Winfrey and Spud Davis. The gray-haired Winfrey was the first rancher to successfully challenge Blunt's claim to all of Pecan Creek. Of the old style, Winfrey never came to town without wearing a suit and tie and never met a woman without tipping his hat. Spud Davis was a likable fellow with a particular taste for potatoes. With his wife, he ran a small ranch and grew potatoes for trade with the town merchants. All the ranchers wore guns at their waists.

The lawyer Yantis shook his head, then stared straight at Hampton. "The sheriff's right."

"What?" Hampton shouted while the others formed a chorus of complaints, staring in disbelief at one another. "You mean," Hampton said, "Blunt and his men can get by with killing two men, and the law's helpless to do anything about it? What the hell's the law for if it can't send men to prison?"

Yantis lifted his hand. "Hear me out."

Gibson pulled his flask from his overalls, uncorked it and offered it around the semicircle of chairs. Everyone declined his offer, bringing a momentary smile to his face.

"Put it away, Let," commanded Hampton. "I want everyone to have a clear head when we discuss this."

His smile evaporating, Gibson grumbled but complied.

The lawyer took a deep breath. "The sheriff's right that we can't prove in a court of law who murdered the Gillyards. The sheriff's lazy and a friend of Blunt's, so you won't get anywhere with him. The district attorney's sympathetic to Blunt, as well, so forcing a prosecution against Blunt is unlikely."

Winfrey lifted his finger toward Yantis. "Just a minute. What you're saying is the law won't do a damn thing and Blunt can pick us off one by one."

Yantis answered with a stare and a cold nod. "The law's only as good as the people charged to enforce it."

Hampton shook his head. "We came here looking for a way within the law to defend ourselves and our property. We all know it wasn't a cyclone or lightning that destroyed the Gillyard place. It was Blunt's dynamite."

Yantis lifted his hand to protest. "Knowing is one thing, but proving in a court of law is another."

"Dammit," shouted Walls, "we just sit back and wait on them to kill us! Is that what you are suggesting?"

The lawyer took two steps and stood over Walls. "As a lawyer, I am not suggesting anything illegal, but you are all smart men. Do what you have to do to protect yourselves."

Hampton leaned forward in his chair. "Are you advocating vigilante justice?"

Yantis studied Hampton. "As a lawyer, I can't. But if in defending your lives and property you come in conflict with the law, I will defend you."

Hampton stood up. "I suppose our visit is over, Lawyer Yantis. What do we owe you for your time?"

"Owe him, hell," cried Gibson, shoving himself up from his chair and shaking his fist at the lawyer. "He didn't tell us anything worth nothing. Matilda could've made as much sense as him, and you all know how little sense her jabbering makes."

"Easy, Let," called Winfrey, reaching over

and grabbing Gibson's arm.

"Calm down," ordered Hampton. "I'll cover the costs. The rest of you get out of here."

Winfrey tugged at Gibson's arm. "Come on, Let."

Still grumbling, Gibson begrudgingly allowed Winfrey to pull him outside, Walls and Davis following and closing the door behind.

"A hothead like that can cause you trouble, especially when he takes to liquor," Yantis warned.

"How much do I owe you?"

"Before all's said and done, you may owe me your life. Right now, you owe me nothing except your silence that this conversation ever took place."

Hampton nodded. "Why risk your neck for us?"

Yantis patted the six-gun belted high on his waist. "In a community of laws, an attorney-at-law should not have to wear one of these. We may have a law-abiding community right now, but we don't have a lawful town, not with inferior men like the sheriff and the district attorney, who bow to the wishes of the powerful or the monied." The lawyer lifted his hand.

Hampton grabbed it and pumped it vigorously, saying nothing more before turning and exiting the office.

The others stood on the walk in the building's narrow shade.

"How much did he charge?" Gibson demanded.

Hampton strode straight for Gibson and stopped six inches from his nose, close enough to smell the liquor on his neighbor's breath. Hampton shoved him against the plank wall of the lawyer's office.

"Hey," protested Gibson, "what's that all about?"

Lifting his finger and pointing it like a gun at Gibson's nose, Hampton answered with a low, menacing growl. "Don't take another drink before we meet again or you're on your own, Let."

"A man can drink when he likes," Gibson protested.

"Not if you're riding with this bunch."

Gibson's shoulders slumped when he saw the others nodding.

Walls turned to Hampton. "What's the plan, Hugh?"

"Let's break up and go our separate ways. No sense raising suspicions by all of us being seen together in town. You can pair off and go to your places; just be on your guard."

"What about you?" asked Winfrey.

"I've business at the mercantile and may lay low until dusk before starting back for the ranch. We'll meet tomorrow night at Let's place. It's about as central a place as we can meet."

"Good enough," said Davis. The others nodded.

"Then get out of here," Hampton said. "The way we're clumped up, one barrel of Lem Blunt's scattergun would take care of us all."

The other men dispersed quickly, leaving Hampton alone in front of the law office. He glanced at the window and saw Yantis staring back. It was a frightening thought that the law, as Yantis had suggested, was only as good or decent as the people who enforced it.

Hampton nodded at Yantis, then marched on down the street toward the mercantile. Having bought supplies last week, he didn't need anything from the merchant, Claude Stanley, except information. Stanley Mercantile was the biggest supplier in Brown and all the surrounding counties. What Claude Stanley didn't have, he could order from Fort Worth or New Orleans or St. Louis.

Stanley Mercantile and its assorted lumber

sheds and storage buildings took up an entire block facing the courthouse square. Hampton ambled that direction, clinging to the narrow shade that gave slim refuge from the searing heat. If rain didn't come soon, the whole county would melt or burn. The people, the animals, even the flies seemed listless and thirsty.

Hampton had stabled his chestnut at a livery to keep the animal well-watered and out of the sun during the day. By leaving town at dusk, Hampton would keep the chestnut from traveling in the searing heat. He tended the horse daily, feeding and watering him, but even so, the dry weather was taking its toll on every living thing.

Turning at the side street fronting the courthouse square, Hampton walked half-way down the block, then entered the wide mercantile building. Claude Stanley's clerks were scattered among the shelves and tables of goods, helping the few customers who still had money or credit to spare. Stanley himself was at the back of the store near the candy jars, fanning himself with a lady's fan and sucking on a peppermint stick. A white-haired man with broad shoulders and hips, Stanley grinned as Hampton approached.

"I wish I owned one of those newfangled ice factories. I figure I could be a rich man by now."

Hampton laughed. "I always thought you were rich."

Stanley pulled the peppermint stick from his mouth. "I let too many operate on credit over the years. Most pay their debts, but there's just enough who think you owe them something that it cuts into your profits substantially." Stanley shoved the peppermint back in his mouth. Without missing a stroke, he swapped the lady's fan to his other hand and pointed to an empty keg.

Hampton slid onto the keg and took off his hat, wiping the perspiration from his forehead. "If you could bottle this heat and save it for winter, Claude, you could sure cut down on your firewood bill."

"If it were just a little thicker, Hugh, I could slice it and send it up North as slabs of hell. Yankee fools up there would buy it. Anyway, Hugh, what can I do for you? Didn't you get your supplies last week?"

"I did, and I'll bring a few head of cattle in to cover the bill," he answered, then slid the keg closer to Stanley. He looked over both shoulders to see if anyone was within hearing range. Certain there wasn't, he spoke again. "I need information this time."

Pulling the peppermint stick from his mouth, Stanley studied Hampton, then bit his lip before speaking. "It's about Lem Blunt and his orders, isn't it?"

"Dynamite, Claude, has he ordered any dynamite?"

"I don't make it my business to ask a man what he's gonna do with his purchases, Hugh, and I don't usually make one man's business another's concern by telling anyone."

Hampton nodded. "I understand, Claude, but people's lives are at stake."

Stanley held up his hand. "I'm saying it ain't usual for me to talk. This is an unusual circumstance. Not for once did I believe the sheriff's story about cyclone and lightning destroying the Gillyard place."

"Blunt's guilty as Judas," Hampton said. "I followed four, maybe five sets of tracks from the Gillyard cabin to his ranch."

Stanley shook his head. "A month ago he received a case of dynamite."

"Thanks, Claude," Hampton said, starting to arise.

The store owner motioned for him to keep his seat. "Another case arrived day before yesterday and he's supposed to pick it up today or tomorrow."

Hampton whistled low. "I don't figure he's gonna be blowing up stumps with the explosives."

"I don't either and it bothers me, but I guess it's no different than selling a man a gun he uses to kill someone. I didn't light the fuse or pull the trigger on any man's life."

Nodding, Hampton started to rise, but once again Stanley motioned for him to keep his seat.

"Blunt may have come to town today for his dynamite," said the merchant.

Hampton twisted slowly around to look. He saw Josie and Charlie Blunt entering the store. As usual, they were dressed like men, each with a gun hanging on her shapely hip.

A couple of the city women in the store lifted their noses in the air and turned away, but the men and the clerks just stared.

"I feel sorry for those two," Stanley offered, "their father raising them as he did and treating them like whores, if what I've heard is true."

Hampton stroked his chin, recalling his visit to the Blunt place and the sheriff's itch that Lem Blunt had Josie scratch. "I figure it's true."

Stanley grimaced. "They're hard-edged. Don't remember them ever buying a dress or anything girlish. Charlie's always liked horehound candy, but Josie don't care for much of anything. Blunt won't let them buy anything for themselves, so I've always let Charlie have a sack of candy and added the cost to something her pa buys."

"Like dynamite."

Stanley nodded. "Like dynamite."

"I'll tell you what, Claude. This time the candy's on me. Charlie watered my horse when the sheriff and I went calling. How about a pound of her favorite and add it to my account?"

Stanley cocked his head. "You sure about this, Hugh? Her pa don't like any fellows being around them, and he'll be by here shortly. He always drops them off, then heads for the saloon for a couple drinks before returning."

Hampton laughed. "Blunt's already threatened to kill me. What difference does this make?"

The store owner shrugged. "Your money, your life." Slowly, he pushed himself up from his rocking chair and retreated behind the counter to a candy jar. He lifted the glass lid and counted out pieces of candy on the scale before replacing the lid. He pulled a strip of brown paper from a giant roll behind the counter and quickly wrapped the candy, tying it up with a length of string. Stanley tossed the package over the counter.

Hampton snatched it from the air.

Stanley leaned over the counter and laughed. "It's on the house, provided she doesn't slap or maim you."

Hampton nodded as he stood up, hat in one hand, candy in the other. Across the store, the two sisters stood with their backs to him, examining leather work gloves commonly used by cowhands.

The wooden floor creaked as he approached. Both women turned around, Josie casting him a haughty look, then tossing a pair of work gloves back on the table and striding off. Charlie's gaze lingered for a moment, a bashful, almost embarrassed smile tugging at the corner of her lips.

Hampton offered her the package. "For watering my horse."

For an instant, she seemed not to understand, as if no one had ever given her a gift. She paused, glancing from his hand to his eyes, then toward Josie.

"It's a thank-you," Hampton smiled, "for watering my horse."

She nodded meekly. "He was thirsty."

"It's horehound candy."

"My favorite."

"Then take it."

Charlie lifted her hands to the package, her fingers brushing against his as she took it. "What do you want for it?"

70

"Nothing."

Slowly, she lifted the package to her breast and lowered her head in embarrassment. "Thank you."

Hampton stepped toward her, raising his hand until his index finger touched her chin. He lifted her chin and smiled, but before he could say anything, he heard a profane commotion at the door.

He twisted to see Lem Blunt charging down the aisle for him.

"What the hell are you doing with my daughter, you son of a bitch?" Blunt screamed, and several customers scrambled for the door. "Trying to turn her against me, are you?" He slapped at the gun at his side, but Charlie lunged toward him.

Hampton lifted the leather catch, then slid his revolver from his holster, cocking the hammer.

"Pa, he gave me candy, that's all. For watering his horse at our place. Don't cause any trouble," she pleaded, holding the package of candy out for him.

He swatted it to the floor, then drew back his arm and slapped her hard across the face.

Charlie screamed as she stumbled into the adjacent table of tin pails and tinware, knocking several pieces to the floor in a clatter. Charlie bounced back toward him, her arms flailing at his gun hand. "Don't draw, Pa, he didn't mean nothing by it." Charlie clamped her hands around his wrist.

Blunt struggled with her a moment until he saw Hampton's Colt staring him in the face. His arm went limp.

Hampton motioned for Blunt to lift his arms.

The rancher hesitated. "Josie, do something to help your pa!"

Hampton glanced quickly at Josie.

"Sure, Pa," she replied, raising her arms so that Hampton understood she was no threat and walking toward her sister. She walked between Hampton and Blunt, then squatted by the scattered tinware.

Hampton suspected a trick, fearing she would go for her gun and he would have to shoot her, then pick off Blunt. Hampton's stomach knotted at the prospect of shooting a woman. He decided to shoot her father first, then see if he could disarm her.

Josie arose slowly, holding her hands away from her waist. In one hand, she held the package of horehound candy. "Here, Charlie, you dropped this. Now let's go out to the wagon and wait."

Charlie grabbed the bundle of candy.

"Wait," Hampton ordered. "One of you

take your pa's pistol."

Josie grabbed his gun as she eased past him.

"You girls'll pay for this when I get you home."

"We're just trying to save you, Pa, that's all," said Josie. "You'd be a fool to jerk leather when he's got a bead on you."

Josie took Charlie's arm and aimed her for the door. In a moment the two sisters were outside, climbing into their wagon.

"You stay away from my girls," Blunt screamed. "You're trying to turn them against me. I know men like you want to bed them down like breeding animals."

Hampton shoved his pistol in his holster and approached the rancher. "You insult me and your daughters." Drawing back his hand, he slapped Blunt across the side of his head. "That's for Charlie."

Blunt cursed and screamed as Hampton backed out the door.

"You're a dead man now, Hampton. I won't forget this until you're rotting in your grave."

6

At dusk Hugh Hampton rode his chestnut out of town and toward his place up Pecan Creek. Though the sun had disappeared, the heat had settled over the land and each breath seared Hampton's lungs. The chestnut was listless and Hampton didn't push the gelding. A mile out of town, Hampton heard a threatening noise and jerked his carbine from its scabbard. Nothing came of it, but he cradled the Henry in the crook of his left arm, ready to defend himself without a moment's hesitation.

When the trail finally brought him within view of his cabin, he tugged on the reins and stopped. "What the hell?" he said to himself as he studied the glow lighting the windows. Someone had visited his cabin and was perhaps still inside. Or had someone set a fire inside? He studied the windows, deciding the even light came from a lamp, not a flame. Twice, he thought he saw the shadow of a figure passing the window.

But where was Andy? The dog wouldn't let someone that close to the house unless the intruder had shot the mongrel. Was it a trap? Hampton shrugged, knowing only one way to find out. He touched the flank of his chestnut with his boot heel and started the animal toward the cabin.

Hampton's index finger slid naturally past the Henry's trigger guard and over the trigger, ready to defend himself or reclaim his cabin. His chestnut moved so listlessly that the gelding made a noiseless advance, allowing Hampton to reach the porch with the certainty that he had not been heard. Hampton eased out of the saddle, its leather creaking as he shifted his weight onto a single stirrup and then slipped to the ground. He took the reins and looped them over the hitching rail, then stepped onto the porch, the wood groaning under his weight.

Inching toward the door, Hampton grimaced at every creak and groan of the dry planks beneath his boot. He smelled the aroma of burning mesquite in the stove. No one would make a fire in this heat unless he was cooking a meal. Reaching the door, Hampton leaned against it and listened. From the other side of the door, Hampton heard Andy's bark. The dog was okay, but the mongrel had given Hampton away. Instantly, he barged inside.

Andy jumped for his legs, glad to see him. In the instant that it took Hampton's eyes to adjust to the light, he heard a voice he recognized.

"I vas vondering vhen you vould be here," came the high-pitched voice that could only belong to Simon Levine, a Jewish peddler who made the rounds of Brown County ranches twice a year. "I make myself at home, do the cooking like a baleboste, feed your dog like he is my own child and vhat thanks do I get but you coming in vith your long gun, pointing it at my face like I'm a meshuggener."

Hampton shook his head and lowered the barrel of the carbine. "How are you, Simon?"

"Much better vhen I see you've put avay your Vinchester rifle."

"Henry," Hampton corrected.

"So, you name your long gun, too? Vhat you goyim do amazes me yet. And, vhere have I not been in Texas? Novhere have I not been in Texas."

Hampton leaned over and patted Andy on the head. The dog shook his head and rubbed against Hampton's leg. "Has Simon talked you to death, Andy?" Hampton moved out of the door and the mongrel darted past him into the dark.

"The dog is smarter than you, Hugh Hampton, because he listens to vhat I have to say. You try to converse, but the dog, he listens and learns, but not you. You try to tell me things."

Hampton laughed. "Simon, I'm surprised I ever have a chance to get a word in, as fast as you talk."

Levine pounded his fist into his palm to accentuate his answer. "Ve Jews know ve must make the best use of our time on earth. Ve must talk fast to get in all ve've got to say, vhich is much."

Hampton leaned his Henry against the wall. "What did you fix me for supper, Simon?"

"Vhat could be better than lentil soup?"

"Nothing when you're cooking, Simon. Did you put a slab of salt pork in to flavor it?"

"Vhat did you say? Vas it pork? You have not learned about us Jews. Ve do not eat pork like goyim."

"Well, Simon, why don't you fix me a bowl of soup while I tend my horse in the barn."

"I vant you to be careful in your barn. Vhy? Because that's vhere I put up my vagon and my matched grays, best horses they are that ever pulled a vagon."

Hampton shook his head. "Where did you put all your money, Simon? I could use a loan."

"Vhat, you think I have money? Vhat foolishness."

"Maybe so, but that's what many in these parts think of you."

"Vhat, that they vere right? Vould I still be traveling from place to place, trying to make a small living for myself? I think not."

Hampton laughed, then stepped back outside, closing the door behind him. Simon Levine was a garrulous but otherwise harmless fellow. He was fine in small doses, like an overnight stay, but Hampton knew his persistent chatter would make a prolonged presence intolerable.

Untying his horse, Hampton headed for the barn, squeezing the chestnut inside between Levine's wagon and the two stalls now holding the matched grays. Hampton unsaddled his gelding in the dark, knowing the routine so well that it was second nature by now. He fed and watered the horse, then started back to the house. As he walked, he occasionally caught glimpses of Andy roaming about the place, looking for intruders.

At the door to his cabin, he took a deep

breath, then entered, prepared to listen to Levine's vocal meanderings.

"Back so soon? Vhat, you not take such good care of your horse as I take of my matched grays? Fine horses, vhich cost me plenty, but they're vorth it. How can people not buy from a vagon pulled by such a fine pair of horses?"

"What about the soup, Simon?"

"It's nearly ready, Hugh Hampton. No place in all my travels vhere I had rather stay than vith you. I vill serve the soup."

Hampton slid into his chair and watched Levine. He was a little man whose movements were herky-jerky, like his speech. He wore thick eyeglasses over owlish eyes. He had a prominent nose over thin lips and crooked teeth. He stood but five feet four inches tall and weighed barely a hundred pounds.

He grinned at Hampton as he set a steaming bowl of soup in his place. He returned a moment later with a bowl of his own and a tin of bland crackers that Hampton remembered from Levine's last visit.

Sitting down at the table, Levine offered a prayer in Hebrew, then picked up his spoon.

"I hope, Simon, you asked for an end to this drought," Hampton said before he spooned a bite of soup. It was flavorful, but nowhere near as filling as he would have preferred after such a long day. "The drought," Hampton asked, "when will it end?"

"Vhen vill it be over? I do not know, but I vish it vould hurry and rain. People aren't buying vhat they used to buy."

"Money's tighter than rain right now."

Levine took a bite of soup, making a big show of how much he liked his own cooking. "Vhat is this but the best soup I have ever cooked?"

Hampton nodded. "Good, but a little thin."

"Thin, vhy that is vhat it should be. I bring you a fine meal and all you do is complain?"

Hampton ate one of the bland crackers, then pointed his finger at Levine. "Next time, bring me rain."

"Vish that I could, so parched is the land, so many animals dying of thirst. Vhat is God trying to tell us? He vill send rains vhen we are right with him, I tell you that. Must be a great evil vhich is over the land."

Perhaps, Hampton thought, the evil was the drought. Or perhaps it was Lemuel Blunt. After more than an hour of listening to Simon Levine's incessant chatter, Hampton arose, stretching his arms and yawning.

"I'm turning in, Simon. You're welcome to stay up and talk to yourself as long as you like," he teased.

"Vhat vith you making funny of me talking. You should be thankful I visit vith you. Not everyone has such luck."

"Not everyone would let you stay with them."

"Nor vould I vant to stay with everyone. I bring my bedroll. I sleep upon your floor."

Hampton laughed. "At least you don't talk in your sleep, Simon."

The peddler lifted his finger and shook it at Hampton. "You vorry too much about my talking. You should vorry more about absorbing my visdom."

"Good night," Hampton said as he marched from the kitchen into the room where he kept his bed. He retired quickly and went to sleep shortly after Levine cleaned the dishes and blew out the lamp.

Come morning, Hampton was up at dawn, tending to his chestnut and the peddler's matched grays. He was harnessing Levine's team when the peddler approached the barn, his bedroll under his arm.

"Vhy I stay with you, Hugh Hampton, is that you alvays ready my team vhen it's time to go. Some might say you only vant to get rid of me as soon as possible." Levine shrugged. "Maybe so, maybe not, but vhatever the reason I still get my team harnessed vithout vork on my part."

Hampton knew Levine would next offer to pay him for sheltering him, his wagon and his team. "Just being neighborly."

Levine lifted the tarpaulin at the back of his wagon and shoved his bedroll in place, then tied the tarp. Turning to Hampton, the peddler reached for the collar of his loose-fitting muslin pullover shirt and grabbed the leather thong that hung around his neck. Levine fished out a large leather pouch with a Star of David carved on the front. "Vell," Levine started, "I must pay you vhat for your hospitality and for the vork you've done with my horses?" He pulled out a wad of greenbacks, tied in a roll with a piece of twine.

Hampton answered with a wave of the arm. "Keep your money, Simon. I don't run a hotel, so you're welcome as a friend."

"Vhatever you say, Hugh Hampton." Levine quickly deposited the money back in the pouch and dropped it inside his shirt. He tugged at his black, flat-brimmed, low-crowned hat.

"One warning, Simon," Hampton began, "about . . ."

"Vhat? Have I offended you or vhatever?"

Hampton shook his head. "The drought has stretched people's nerves and wallets pretty tight. Don't let many folks see your money pouch or harm might come to you."

"Vhat am I but a poor peddler? People think I am rich, do they? Vould a rich man travel in such hot veather on dusty roads vith a vagonload of goods to sell? No, he vould have a mansion."

"It doesn't matter if you're rich or not, Simon. If someone thinks you are, he could harm you just the same, steal what money you have."

Levine clutched at the pouch beneath his shirt.

Hampton led the harnessed grays in front of the wagon, then backed them over the wagon tongue to hook them up. "And one other thing, Simon. You best avoid the Blunt place."

"Vhy is that? Lemuel Blunt buys plenty, though he is none too friendly."

"The drought's stretched him thinnest of all. He's become so desperate he's threatened people. Some of us think he dynamited the Gillyard brothers."

Levine stroked his scraggly beard. "The vay selling is, I must visit whoever buys. I do not like Blunt. Once he offered me either of his daughters in exchange for vhatever he vanted from my vagon. I tell him I trade for cash, nothing else vhatsoever. I feel sorry for his daughters both."

Hampton nodded, thinking back to the previous day and how Blunt had slapped Charlie in Stanley Mercantile. After he finished hooking up the team, he stretched the reins from the harness to the wagon seat, then led the horses outside, the wagon rattling and creaking as it moved. Once the wagon cleared the barn, Hampton stopped the horses and set the brake.

"You're ready, Simon."

"You are a good Gentile, Hugh Hampton." Levine offered Hampton his hand.

Levine's grasp was weak, but Hampton shook it warmly. "Wish you'd promise me you'd not go near the Blunt place on this trip, Simon."

Levine shrugged. "Vhat's a peddler to do but to try to make a living? Several ranches I must visit or people vill think me not dependable, but I'll be in town in a couple days to sell Claude Stanley some items."

Hampton patted Levine on the back, knowing the peddler was too stubborn to change his mind. "You be careful, Simon, and don't make any campfires that would burn up Brown County."

"That I von't do," he said, stepping on

the wagon wheel and pulling himself into the seat. "Vhy is it you buy nothing this trip?"

"I'm broke, Simon. My cattle are dying, my grass is wilting and I don't have any free money. Feeding and watering your horses cost me the things that even money can't buy right now."

"I vill pay a good man like you vhatever you say, Hugh Hampton." Levine frowned and fished for his money pouch.

Hampton held up his hand. "That's not what I meant, Simon. After all, you paid me for the feed and water last night."

"Vith what?"

"With all your wise talk!"

Levine laughed and slapped the reins against the rumps of his grays. "Then you are a rich man indeed."

Hampton nodded as Levine drove away.

7

The ride toward Let Gibson's place was as discouraging as any Hugh Hampton had ever made. He traversed his fifteen-hundred-acre spread in the hour before dusk and counted a half-dozen dead cattle splayed and bloated in the heat. Buzzards and coyotes were still living well because of the drought, but little else had benefited.

The cattle still on their feet watched with sad, hollow eyes as Hampton rode by. The cattle's ribs were visible under their hides. More cattle would die in a matter of days, or at most weeks, because the yellow, wilted grass that helped them cling to life was disappearing. Without grass to hold the soil together, the ground beneath their sharp hooves was being pulverized. When the cattle moved, their hooves sent up little clouds of dust. Occasionally, a steer would bellow out a lament, then paw at the ground, kicking up more dust. Maybe tomorrow or the next day Hampton would drive half a dozen of the better animals to town and give them to Claude Stanley to settle Hampton's account at the mercantile. Stanley could sell them to the butcher or make some type of deal for him.

Hampton had begun to think he was a poor rancher until he rode onto Let Gibson's place just as the sun dipped below the western horizon. The land and the livestock were no better, everything showing the effects of heat and thirst. He was glad when darkness set in, not just because it brought slight relief from the heat, but also because it brought respite from the terrible sight of land and animals dying before his eyes as he neared Gibson's place.

Through the trees that stood like apparitions along the trail, he could make out the flicker of lights coming from the house. When Hampton cleared the clump of trees, he saw the horses of the other ranchers hitched outside.

As he neared the stone house, he could hear the voices of his neighbors arguing their options against Blunt. They seemed oblivious to everything else, especially the possibility that someone, potentially an enemy, might be approaching. Careless men became jumpy men when they were surprised. Even though they were expecting him, one might panic at the sudden sound of someone outside. Hampton identified himself. "Hello the house," he called. "It's Hugh Hampton."

The discussion went silent and the silhouettes of three men appeared at the two front windows.

"I'm riding in," Hampton called as he steered the chestnut toward the other horses.

Two men emerged from the house, then melded into the darkness.

"Glad you could make it," called Let Gibson. "Matilda was getting worried about you."

"She should've been worried about you," Hampton answered as he halted the gelding in front of the hitching rail.

"What do you mean?" Gibson shot back.

Dismounting, Hampton took the reins and looped them around the rail. "For all the noise you fellows were making, it wouldn't have taken a Comanche to sneak up and shoot you."

"We got a little careless," said Frank Winfrey from the darkness of the porch.

"If we're on our own, we can't be careless again or one of us could get hurt," Hampton chided. He made out a form that was

Winfrey and clasped his outstretched hand before moving to Gibson and greeting him.

Gibson motioned for Hampton to step inside. As Hampton entered, he was greeted by Spud Davis, Johnny Walls and Matilda Gibson, who gave him a big hug. Matilda was a portly woman with a generosity and spirit as wide as her girth. She had to be a forgiving woman to have lived all her married life with Let Gibson.

"You're looking as fine as ever, Matilda," Hampton said.

Matilda stepped back, her hands on her abundant hips, and studied him. "I still can't figure why a man as handsome as you still lives alone in that cabin."

"Alone? Why, I've got Andy."

Matilda shook her head. "That's the ugliest mongrel I ever laid eyes on . . . too much coyote blood in him. You need someone to fix your meals and take care of you."

Hampton nodded. "Just last night I had such a person, Matilda. Made my supper and did my dishes."

Matilda cocked her head suddenly, as if she were unsure whether she should be pleased or shocked by this announcement. Her smile slowly drained from her face. "Who was she?"

"She? Who said anything about she,"

89

Hampton laughed. "It was Simon Levine."

The smile bloomed again on her face and she laughed, slapping her thick thighs through the thin cotton skirt and apron. "No wonder you're late. That old fool could talk the ears off a corn patch, but better you than us."

Let Gibson cleared his throat. "We've matters to discuss, Matilda."

She shook her index finger at his nose. "Hugh Hampton is company in my house and I intend to greet him and show him a little hospitality."

Chastised, Let Gibson moved out of reach of his wife.

Matilda smiled smugly at Hampton. "There's been plenty bad to come out of the Gillyard killings, but one good. Since you put the fear of God in Let about his drinking, he's been drier than a Baptist with lockjaw."

Gibson lowered his head. "And to think some people been saying women should be allowed to vote."

Matilda ignored him. "I made a good pecan pie and saved you the biggest piece as thanks for sobering up my husband. How about a slice and a cup of coffee?"

"Sounds better than Simon Levine's cooking."

"If it isn't, you better not say so." She spun around and went into the kitchen.

Let Gibson groused, "It's about time."

"I heard that," Matilda called.

Gibson shook his head in defeat.

Winfrey motioned for everyone to take a seat, then turned to Hampton. "We were having a spirited discussion on what to do."

"I heard part of it from a half-mile away," Hugh answered. "After I finish my pie, maybe we should step outside to discuss things. There's less temptation outside to let our voices get too loud."

Gibson shook his head. "Matilda will be mad that she can't eavesdrop."

Hampton grinned. "She can join us, Let, as far as I'm concerned."

"This is man's talk," Gibson shot back.

"She's in just as much danger as you if Blunt and his men come calling."

Gibson pursed his lips and nodded. "More danger," he admitted. "She makes a wider target."

"I heard that," Matilda snarled as she returned with a plate of pie and bone-china cup of coffee. She headed straight for Hampton, her voice softening when he took the food offering. "Do enjoy."

Hampton sat down in a kitchen chair that had been moved into the parlor to accommodate everyone. He slid the coffee cup between his legs and began to eat the pecan pie, nodding at its flavor. "Fine pie, Matilda, fine pie."

She answered with a grin.

After downing a bite, Hampton pointed a fork at her. "Once I'm done, we'll carry our chairs outside to discuss our business. You're welcome to join us."

Her husband grumbled.

Hampton grinned. "We took a vote and four out of the five agreed you could listen."

Everyone laughed but Gibson, especially when Matilda spoke. "I wonder who voted against me," she said, staring straight at her husband.

Let Gibson stood up. "Think I'm gonna take my chair on outside right now."

Hampton took a healthy swig of the coffee, then polished off the pie as the others began to take their chairs out the door.

He had no more than finished than Matilda took his plate and cup. "You men talk outside and I'll kill the lamps. No sense wasting coal oil or heating up the house any more than God's already done today."

"Thanks, Matilda."

"No, thank you," she replied, "for scaring Let off of the whiskey for now."

Hampton leaned forward and stood up,

taking the straight-backed chair out the door and carrying it beyond the horses to the circle of men he would've been unable to find without the sound of their voices giving him a clue. He added his chair to the circle, straddled it backwards and rested his arms over the backrest. "What have you fellows decided?"

"That Spencer Yantis ain't much of a lawyer," Gibson said stridently.

"At least we know he's honest," Hampton shot back. "He could've taken our money with no better result."

Winfrey spoke up. "We haven't reached a decision, Hugh. We're damned if we do and damned if we don't."

"That's right," interjected Davis. "If we take the law into our own hands now, we may wind up dead at the end of the noose. If we wait until Blunt attacks again, another of us could be dead."

"The way I figure it," Walls began, "once Blunt got away with the Gillyard murders, he thinks he can get away with anything. I figure we ought to move first, kill him and his whole crew, blow up his damn place like he did the Gillyards', wipe out all of them."

"If we don't," Winfrey said, "they'll pick us off, one by one."

Gibson chimed in. "That Blunt ranch is a

den of rattlesnakes."

Spud Davis coughed nervously. "Boys, the one thing that bothers me is Blunt's two girls."

"Girls, hell!" shot back Gibson. "They carry guns, ride like men and damn sure cuss like them."

"It doesn't matter," Davis answered. "Something in my nature's just against shooting a female."

Hampton let out a slow breath, relieved someone else was squeamish about possibly harming the sisters. "I'm with Spud," Hampton said. "I don't want to hurt the two of them. We all know they haven't had a fair life. Even Simon Levine said Blunt offered them to him as barter goods for trade. They're scared to leave for fear he might kill them."

"Fine, Hugh," said Winfrey. "We'll try not to hurt the females, but there's still Lem Blunt and those four hands. They're a mean crew and we'll have our hands full up against them all, even with your fine shooting abilities."

Hampton replied, "I've a feeling we don't need to get them all. Just one."

"What do you mean?" Gibson asked.

"Blunt's the toughest nut. The rest are followers. If we can get Blunt, then the others may fear for their own lives and drift away."

Walls stood up. "I figure we need to hang him if we can. That'll send a stronger message to his men than just bushwhacking him."

"Shooting him may be hard enough," Hampton said. "We need to catch him alone, identify some habit of his where we can surprise him away from his cabin."

Davis hit his fist against his palm. "I don't know, Hugh. That means somebody's gonna have to spy on his place. Any one of us that he finds is as good as dead."

"That's what he's threatened, but it's no riskier than staying on our own places," Hampton answered. "Blunt knows where to find us. He might not figure we'd be within gunshot of his place. And, there are a few decent hills around the place where you would have a vantage point for observation. Does anybody have any field glasses?"

Nobody answered.

Hampton nodded. "I've got to drive a few head of cattle to town to settle some debts with Claude Stanley. I'll do it tomorrow, see if he has a pair for sale. Who can watch tomorrow?"

Walls volunteered. "I'll do it. When do you think is the best time of day to watch him?"

Hampton stroked his chin as he stood

from his chair. "Try late afternoon, early evening, until dusk. If we corner him and kill him, darkness will help cover our tracks. Who'll take the next night?"

Gibson volunteered. "I'm the closest to your place. I can pick up the field glasses, then pass them on."

"I'll take the next day," Davis offered.

"And me the following," said Winfrey.

"That leaves me the fifth day," Hampton acknowledged. "By then, perhaps we'll know how to get him. And boys, be careful. I know for fact that Blunt bought a case of dynamite last month and picked up another one yesterday at Stanley's Mercantile."

"The son of a bitch," scowled Gibson.

"He's due to get his," Walls added.

"I'm riding back home to protect my place tonight," Hampton said. "Does the same go for the rest of you?"

"We've too much at stake not to look after it," Davis replied.

"Then be careful," Hampton said. "And remember, we aren't going to kill the Blunt women."

"Unless they come gunning for us," Gibson said.

"Unless they come gunning for us," Hampton reluctantly repeated.

8

The six steers were the best he had found on his place, but they were awfully scrawny, their ribs showing, their heads drooping, their eyes listless as their stride. Hugh Hampton was embarrassed to be driving them down town streets. Though nobody had any better animals because of the drought, that didn't soothe Hampton's pride.

Hampton glanced up at the western sky, looking for a cloud that could bring a bit of shade from the afternoon sun. The scorching heat seared his face, and in the distance the broken hills seemed to shimmer and the trees across them seemed to dance in the waves of heat. Hampton's throat was dry as chalk. Taking on Lemuel Blunt was one thing, but how did a man deal with a drought? Suffer, Hampton thought, along with the animals.

Passing the courthouse square, Hampton

turned the six gangly steers down the street leading to the livery stable. He would pen the livestock there so Claude Stanley could inspect them and credit their worth to Hampton's account at the mercantile. As he passed the sheriff's office and jail across the street from the back of the courthouse, Hampton saw Sheriff Perry Johns emerge from the stone building, a cigarette dangling from his lips. Seeing Hampton, the sheriff touched the brim of his hat, then cast a sneering smile. In the deriding gesture, Hampton saw not only a mockery of himself, but also a mockery of the law. Damn him!

Ignoring the sheriff, Hampton touched the heel of his boot to the chestnut and the horse danced ahead of the six beeves, which trod along, kicking up dust with their hooves. At the stables, Hampton called to the liveryman and explained what he wanted. The shirtless stableman, his chest muscled and bronzed, pointed to a pen, then jogged that direction to unlatch the gate. Hampton turned the beeves toward the open gate.

"Hi-yah," Hampton yelled, then whistled, and the steers trotted into the pen, the liveryman closing and latching the gate behind them. Hampton climbed out of the saddle and tossed his reins to the livery-man. "Feed and water him, same as usual."

"Cost has gone up," the liveryman replied.

"How much?"

"Double. The drought and all's the cause."

"Go ahead, as long as my credit is still good."

The liveryman nodded. "I trust you more than most, though the drought's gonna break us all."

As Hampton turned to leave, he noticed a pair of matched grays in the back pen. So, Simon Levine had made it to town okay. Being as talkative and pushy as he was, Levine wasn't the most-liked peddler who ever passed through, but he had a decent and trusting streak in him that wasn't always found in peddlers and drummers.

Hampton strode back to the street, circling wide of the jail to reduce the likelihood of another chance encounter with the sheriff and then heading for Stanley's Mercantile.

The doors and windows were open to the stone building. On the steps sat a couple sweating clerks, enjoying the narrow shade and fanning themselves with a folded news-paper. Hampton stepped to the door. "Stanley around?"

A chalky-faced youth in a white apron jerked his thumb over his shoulder. "Inside, sweating like the rest of us."

Hampton entered and saw Stanley drowsily fanning himself in a rocking chair by the back door. The storekeeper made an effort to arise, but Hampton motioned for him to keep his seat.

"You're the first customer I've had all afternoon," Stanley said. "Nobody wants to get out in the heat." Stanley's face glistened with perspiration. "I figured we could open up all the windows and doors and maybe start us a breeze, but I can't get any more breeze than I can get customers. Now I know you came by for something other than the shade."

Hampton nodded. "I left six beeves down at the stables. They're the best of a declining herd. Figured I could sell them to you to help settle my account."

"Can't give you a good price, Hugh, you understand that?"

"I'll take what you can give me."

"That's what most folks are doing," Stanley admitted.

"I suppose everybody's bartering scrawny beeves to pay you off."

Stanley nodded. "All but one rancher, you'll be surprised to know." The merchant paused, gauging Hampton. "Last I heard he was strapped for money, but I'll be damned if Lem Blunt didn't come in this morning and settle up his account. He flashed a roll of bills bigger than I've seen around these parts in years."

"He likely stole it," Hampton answered.

"But from who? You don't think the Gillyard brothers had any money cached somewhere, do you?"

"If they did, Blunt would've had no way of finding out about it. He was the only one of their neighbors they wouldn't let water stock at their dam. He never forgave them for that and likely killed them because of it."

Stanley's hand trembled as he spoke. "He hasn't forgotten about you giving candy to Charlie. He says you planned to ruin her and he's going to get even. I expect he means it, Hugh."

"I'll be prepared," Hampton responded. "By the way, you got any field glasses?"

Stanley stared at Hampton for a moment. "A little preparation, is it?" The store owner laughed as he pushed himself up from his rocking chair and made his way slowly to the glass-encased gun counter. Stanley spoke as he bent down and unlocked the case. "I've got a good pair with leather case and strap and a lesser pair without."

"Let me see the better pair."

As Stanley straightened and handed him the case, the salesman in him kicked in. "It's equipped with two-and-a-quarter-inch achromatic lenses. It weighs just under three pounds, not counting the case, and is as good a pair as you'll find in all of Brown County. Cost is ten eighty-five, but I'll let you have it for ten dollars."

Hampton weighed the feel of the glasses in his hand, then held them up to his eyes, looking out the window and across the street to the courthouse, all the time adjusting the focus wheel to bring the glasses into focus. "You're beginning to sound like Simon Levine," Hampton teased.

"Yeah, I expect to be seeing him anytime. This is always the first place he stops."

Hampton jerked the glasses from his eyes and twisted his head around to gauge Stanley. "Levine hasn't been by to see you?"

The merchant lifted his arms and turned his hands toward Hampton. "No, why?"

"Levine's matched grays are at the stable."

"No one has mentioned seeing him, and his rig is not easy to miss."

Hampton gritted his teeth, then shook his head. "You say Lem Blunt came in today and paid off his account from a wad of bills?"

"That's as right as the weather is dry. You

don't think he murdered him, do you?"

"I don't know," Hampton answered, shoving the field glasses back in the case, "but I intend to find out." He offered the case to Stanley, but the merchant waved it away.

"Take it and I'll add it to your account."

Hampton strode out the front door and back down the street toward the stables. The few people braving the heat of the day shook their heads at his rapid gait, then went about their business. He had to find out about the grays without creating too much suspicion, so he forced himself to walk slower. As he approached the livery stable and pens, he took a couple deep breaths and looked for the liveryman. Not spotting him, Hampton made for the wide stable door, opening it and sliding inside. He breathed in the aroma of fresh manure and stale hay.

"Over here in the back stall," the liveryman called.

Hampton eased that direction. He held up the leather case with the field glasses. "Just bought these and wanted to leave them with my gear."

"Sure thing," the liveryman said. "I'm watering your horse now."

Hampton stopped behind his chestnut in the back stall and handed the case to the liveryman, who draped the strap over the saddle horn.

"Don't forget to tie it down better when you leave," the liveryman warned. "Anything else I can do for you?"

Hampton nodded. "I just noticed that pair of matched grays out in the pen. Fine-looking pair of animals."

"They are indeed," the liveryman answered, turning around to face Hampton. "Lem Blunt sold them to me this morning, saying he hated to part with them but he needed to pay off his account at the mercantile. You interested in buying them?"

Letting out a slow breath, Hampton shook his head. He knew Simon Levine was dead and Lem Blunt, or his men, had killed the peddler. "I don't have the money right now. The drought's drained the lifeblood out of me and a lot of other things," Hampton said as he turned away.

How could he prove what he knew in his heart? How could he make the law work like it should against Lem Blunt? Was the drought going to ruin Brown County first? Or was Lem Blunt? Hampton had more questions than answers. He paused at the stable door, debating whether to return for his horse and just ride away or go to the sheriff. Though he doubted the chance for success, he knew he must give the law one more opportunity to work.

He emerged from the stable and aimed straight for the sheriff's office. His anger was as hot as the afternoon sun by the time he reached the jail. He twisted the door handle and shoved the door open. The sheriff was seated at his desk, fanning himself with his hat.

"What's your problem this time, Hugh?"

"Same thing as last time, Sheriff, and it's not a cyclone or a lightning strike."

Perry Johns picked up a smoldering cigarette from a tin tray and began to suckle on the smoke. "I don't reckon I follow you."

"Lem Blunt's the problem. You and I both know he killed the Gillyard brothers, though only one of us will admit it. Now he's killed Simon Levine."

"The Jewish peddler? Why, I ain't seen him in six months or more and you're saying Blunt killed him?"

Hampton nodded. "He was at my house night before last."

"Then, whoa, Hugh. If you saw him last, how do know you didn't kill him?"

"Hear me out."

"Okay, but you may be digging yourself a hole you can't get out of."

"Levine drove a team of matched grays, a team that's at the livery stable now. The liveryman said Lem Blunt brought them in this morning and sold him the two grays."

The sheriff let out a long, slow breath full of cigarette smoke. "I see what you mean, Hugh. Maybe I misjudged your accusations. The law can't assume many things, but it seems there's more coincidences here than should be. Sounds to me like it's serious enough to take up with the county attorney, see if he might consider an indictment."

Hampton was shocked and pleased at the sheriff's response. Finally, the law was reacting the way it should.

"Take a seat, Hugh, while I run across the street and see if Royce Dugan is in his office. He may be interested in asking you a few questions." As the sheriff stood, he motioned to a bench against the wall. "Wait there under the window, catch what breeze you can. I'll be back in five minutes, maybe less."

As Perry Johns quickly moved out the door and across the street, Hampton wondered what had come over the sheriff. Had the pin on the badge at his chest pricked his conscience, or had Hampton's persistence in exposing Blunt for the evil man that he was finally taken its toll? Hampton was pleased with himself, even more so when the sheriff returned.

"Dugan wants to see you quick, if you've got the time."

Hampton nodded. "I've got all the time it takes." He felt confident and pleased with himself. He had given the law another chance and it had worked. Now he questioned the lawyer Yantis's advice and wondered if Yantis was merely trying to get them to commit a crime so he could make money defending them.

Quickly, Hampton followed Johns out the door, across the street and up the stairs of the stone courthouse. At the head of the stairs, they marched down a narrow wooden hallway toward a man standing at an office door. Though he had never met Dugan, Hampton recognized him by sight.

"Afternoon," Hampton said, offering the attorney his hand. "I'm Hugh Hampton."

Royce Dugan was a short, thin man with cold, calculating eyes. Instead of shaking Hampton's hand, he opened the office door and went inside. "Come on in, Mr. Hampton," Dugan sneered, "because I'd like you to . . ."

Dismayed by the attorney's frigid demeanor, Hampton looked at the sheriff, who nodded his head for him to enter. As Hampton stepped across the threshold, he saw another man and heard Dugan finish his sentence.

". . . meet my friend, Lem Blunt."

Hampton was stunned, his hand falling instinctively to his gun until he felt the press of the sheriff's gun in his back.

"Now," the sheriff growled, "what was it you were saying about Royce Dugan's good friend Lem Blunt?"

"Son of a bitch," Blunt shouted across the room, then licked his thin lips and scratched his unruly beard. "You stay away from my daughters. You've no business giving them candy."

Dugan held up his hand. "Shut up, Lem, let's see what kind of nerve your neighbor has. He's been spreading rumors behind your back. Now tell us, Mr. Hampton, what it was you told the sheriff."

Johns jammed the barrel of his gun hard against Hampton's back and he stumbled a step toward Dugan and Blunt.

"You know what's going on here. Blunt killed Simon Levine, stole the grays and brought them into town to sell."

Dugan slammed his balled fist against the desk "Is that a fact, Mr. Hampton? The law operates on fact, not on supposition. Have you Mr. Levine's body? Have you any witnesses? Have you anything to support your accusations other than your hatred for Mr. Blunt?"

Hampton hesitated until the sheriff jabbed him in the back with his gun. "Not yet."

"I thought not," Dugan replied, then turned to Blunt. "There's another side to all the confusion you have generated. Now, Lem, tell Mr. Hampton what happened."

Blunt wiped his hand across his beard and licked his thin lips like a wolf eyeing a trapped rabbit. "That Jew fellow came by my place, saying business was bad and he was getting out. Wanted to know if I would buy his rig and horses, all his belongings. My girls thought there was a lot of useful things in his wagon, so I paid him a fair price and threw in a saddle horse and old saddle for him to ride out of the county on. He said the drought had killed business."

Hampton shook his head. "That's not proof."

"Very good, Mr. Hampton," said the lawyer. "Now, Lem, show him the proof."

Blunt sneered again. "Son of a bitch," he said as he stuck his hand in his britches pocket. He fished from his pants a leather pouch with long leather ties.

Hampton caught a glimpse of the pouch and bit his lip. Carved in the leather was a Star of David. The pouch had been Simon

Levine's. The Jewish peddler was surely dead, and Blunt had paid off his mercantile account with Levine's money.

Blunt untied the leather thong and pulled open the pouch's mouth. With his thumb and index finger he dug out a piece of compactly folded paper and handed it to Dugan.

The attorney unfolded it and held it out to Hampton for inspection. "This," said Dugan, "is a receipt for the sale of Simon Levine's wagon, goods and horses, signed in his signature."

Hampton shook his head. "Is it signed in his blood, too?"

His comment drew another jab of the sheriff's pistol barrel.

Gritting his teeth, Hampton challenged the trio. "If Levine signed it, he was forced to before he died."

"Shut up," the attorney commanded, "and listen. I'll let you leave here today, but you better keep your wrong opinions to yourself or you'll be in a lot more trouble than you can imagine."

The sheriff eased from behind Hampton, but kept his revolver pointed at his chest.

Dugan shook his fist at Hampton. "A man that tells as many lies as you won't keep friends in Brown County. You better think about keeping your mouth shut or moving on."

Hampton nodded. "I've learned all I need to know."

Dugan shook his head. "You won't get many more lessons so make the most of this one."

Blunt lifted Levine's money pouch where Hampton could see the Star of David. Slowly he jerked the leather pouch shut, as if he were strangling an enemy. "You better stay away from my daughters, you son of a bitch."

Dugan nodded. "You better listen to my friend Lem," he threatened. "Or I just might have to see to it that you are indicted for rape."

The sheriff laughed.

Hampton backed to the threshold, grabbed the door, slammed it shut and bolted down the hall. In his wake he could hear the laughter of Blunt, the county attorney and the sheriff. He ran down the stairs and out onto the courthouse lawn, its grass as patchy as the morals of the county attorney and sheriff.

The lawyer Yantis had been right after all.

Hampton realized his hands were shaking and his knees were mushy. He had known fear on occasion throughout his life, but never like this. It was not that these men were any meaner than others he had faced, but that they were more sinister because of the positions of trust they held. Law gone bad was worse than no law at all. He could expect no justice from the law as practiced in Brown County.

Hampton would have to make his own law on his own terms.

Or he would have to run from Brown County!

He was not running.

9

"You look pale," said Matilda Gibson. "Is it the heat?"

Hugh Hampton shook his head. "More trouble. Is Let about?"

"Somewhere," she replied. "I'll fetch him; you just take a seat and rest yourself."

Matilda scurried from the parlor and out the back door, yelling for her husband.

In a moment, he heard Let's shout from the barn. "What's the trouble?" He yelled, "I'm coming with my gun."

"It's Hugh," she called.

"Dammit, no, nothing's happened to him, has it?"

"No," Matilda yelled. "He's here to see you."

Gibson bounded through the back door, gasping for breath and grumbling at his exasperating wife. He barged into the parlor.

Hampton offered Gibson an explanation and the case with the field glasses. "Bad run-in with Blunt, the sheriff and Royce Dugan."

Gibson whistled. "The county attorney."

"He's in this with the sheriff and Blunt," Hampton stated. "What the lawyer Yantis suggested is true. The law'll be no help, Let. We're in this on our own."

Gibson shook his head.

"To make matters worse, I think Blunt killed Simon Levine."

Matilda came in from the kitchen carrying a glass of water. "Oh, no," she gasped. "Simon was harmless and didn't deserve that." She handed the water to Hampton.

Taking the glass, he nodded. "Blunt sold Levine's matched grays to the livery stable this morning and paid off his account at the mercantile. I saw him carrying Levine's money pouch."

Gibson lowered his head into his open palms, then ran his fingers through his hair. "Did you take it up with the sheriff?"

Hampton gulped down the water. "That's when I met Dugan." He detailed the meeting in the county attorney's office.

Shaking his head, Gibson took a seat, his wife moving to his side and patting him on the leg as they listened.

"The law's gone bad in Brown County," Hampton said, "and there's nothing we can do about it without breaking the law."

Gibson looked at Matilda. "Maybe I should send you away for a few weeks, visit your sister."

"No," she answered emphatically. "I'll not abandon you now. We stood off Comanche when we were younger and we'll stand off the law now, if that's what it takes."

"Damn them to hell," Gibson said.

Hampton stood up and handed Matilda the empty glass. "I best get to my place."

Matilda jumped up and hugged Hampton. "You be careful, all by yourself. At least Let's got me. He thinks I make a big target, but I can shoot as well as he can." She released him and scurried to the kitchen, returning in a moment with a clean kerchief tied at the corners. "There's two pieces of fried steak and some cold taters you can eat, save you having to worry about supper."

"Obliged, Matilda," Hampton said, leaning over and kissing her on the cheek.

With the field glasses in his left hand, Gibson put his right hand on Hampton's shoulder as he walked out onto the front porch. "Be careful."

Hampton nodded, knowing that a man could be only so careful and then luck — or God — came into play. He packed the bundle of food in his saddlebag, then mounted up. "The field glasses, Let — use them tomorrow, then swap off. Maybe we can kill Lem Blunt without making a blood-bath of it all."

"I'll do my best, Hugh, and you watch out for yourself. After what happened today, I figure they'll come for you first."

That was the way Hampton read the cards, but he didn't admit it as he turned the chestnut toward home. He lifted the leather catch off the hammer of the pistol on his left hip and rode away, jumpy the entire journey, his hands sweaty not just from the oppressive heat but from his nerves as well. As his gelding approached a clump of prickly pear, a solitary quail exploded from beneath the cactus. Hampton jerked his pistol free and had the hammer cocked before he recognized what had startled him. He slid the pistol back in his holster.

To the west, as the sun sank, the distant sky had turned red, like the blood that had been spilled in Brown County. Hampton wondered if his own blood would soon ir-rigate the dry soil of the place he called home.

As he came within sight of the cabin, he pulled his Henry carbine from its scabbard and cradled it in the crook of his elbow. He approached the cabin cautiously and hid for ten minutes in a thicket of live oak, studying the place for any sign that something was amiss. At first he didn't see Andy, but then the dog ambled around the corner of the house and took up his favorite spot on the porch.

Reassured by the sight of the dog, he emerged from the trees and directed the chestnut toward the barn. Hampton was still better than a hundred yards away when Andy heard his approach and loped off the porch to greet him.

Hampton nudged the chestnut into a trot and Andy barked his greetings. "Howdy, Andy," Hampton answered, shoving his carbine back in its scabbard. "Good job, boy! Think you can keep guard during the night?" Hampton dismounted, grabbing Andy by the neck and shaking him playfully. The dog growled, then rolled over on his back for a moment before jumping onto his feet and trotting to the barn.

Hampton led his gelding into the barn and worked quickly to unsaddle him, feed and water him. Hampton noted his water barrel was low in the barn and realized he would have to tote water from the cistern to fill it tomorrow. He grabbed his carbine and lifted the flap on his saddlebag to retrieve the bundle of food Matilda had provided. As he removed the food, his hand brushed against the Bible he had picked up from the debris at the Gillyard place the day after the bombing. Andy caught the scent of the meat and potatoes and lunged for Hampton's hand. Hampton jerked it away.

"I'll share with you, boy, if you just wait a minute. I know you're hungry, but so am I."

Andy attentively followed Hampton to the cabin, then jumped inside the moment Hampton opened the door. The cabin was hot and stuffy. Hampton placed the carbine on the kitchen table, then untied the kerchief and took a piece of fried steak and tossed it to Andy. The dog ate it greedily while Hampton alternated bites of potato with the remaining piece of meat.

As soon as Andy swallowed his meat, he was at Hampton's side, barking for more. Hampton offered him a potato, which he gobbled down as well, finishing before Hampton had consumed half of his piece of fried meat. Andy licked his teeth anxiously and Hampton finally gave in, dropping the last of the meat to his mouth. Hampton finished the remainder of his potato and the one remaining on the kerchief. By the time he was done, he was barely able to see in the dimness of nightfall.

Hampton opted not to light a lamp, figuring this would be a dangerous night. There was no point in giving potential enemies a shot at his profile through a window. He groped for two boxes of cartridges from a shelf by the door and carried them and his carbine into the bedroom.

Returning to the kitchen, he made out Andy standing on his hind legs over the table, checking for more meat in the kerchief.

"Down, Andy, down."

The dog jumped down from the table and ambled for the door. Hampton opened it and let him outside. "Stay alert, Andy," he called as he barred the door.

Hampton slipped back to his bed, a low-slung wooden frame with crisscrossed rope supporting a thin cotton mattress. It was a double mattress, which he had bought with expectations of one day having a wife. But life had never fulfilled those expectations. He envied Let Gibson for his Matilda. She was not the best-looking woman in the world, but she cared for Let and fried him meat and boiled him potatoes and let him share a bed with her. And now, when Let was in danger, there was someone who was willing to stand with him. Andy was a poor substitute for a woman.

Taking off his hat, he tossed it at the chair in the corner, then placed his carbine on the floor at the side of the bed where he could find it should trouble come. He pulled off his boots and placed them beside the carbine, then shoved a box of cartridges in each. In case of trouble, he could grab the carbine and his two boots and escape with enough ammunition to make a fight of it. He decided to sleep in his gun belt, so he hooked the leather catch over the hammer of his Colt .45. Now there was nothing to do but wait or sleep.

He crawled into bed atop the sheets. He stiffened at the sound of Andy's bark, then relaxed when the dog quieted. Hampton had never felt jumpier. He had to admit to himself that the incident in the county attorney's office had rattled him. The confidence and the gall of the county attorney in abusing the law sickened him. Lem Blunt had gotten away with murder, and the two men responsible for seeing that justice was done had merely winked at the crime.

Not only that, they had as much as threatened to bring him up on rape charges if he kept prying into Blunt's affairs. The irony of that possibility sickened him, because the whole county knew how Lem Blunt used his daughters for other men's pleasure — if not his own.

Hampton tossed in the bed, plagued by the fears that kept running through his mind. Johns and Dugan could destroy his good name. He had striven over the years to be an honest, decent man and thought he was liked and respected in Brown County. Now two men toyed with his reputation as gleefully as a cat plays with a mouse before killing it. He felt sweat beading all over his body.

Eventually, the worries — if not the heat — faded away, and he drifted off into a restless, intermittent sleep filled with interruptions, all imagined except one. Well after midnight he twisted in his bed, then shot upright at the sound of Andy's furious barking.

His enemies had come!

He threw his legs over the side of the bed, grabbing his boots and extracting the cartridge box from each one before shoving his feet inside. As he stood, he jammed the cartridge boxes in his pants pockets, then bent to pick up his carbine.

Andy growled and spit at some intruder behind the cabin, toward Pecan Creek.

Hampton glanced out the window. The night was moonless and pitch-dark. The darkness would help him get outside without being spotted, but it would also provide cover for the potential assassins.

Andy barked furiously, apparently running back and forth between the ends of the cabin.

Hampton slipped from the bedroom into the kitchen. Quietly, quickly, he unbarred the door, then lifted the latch and slipped outside onto the porch.

His luck held because he drew no gunshots. "Andy," he whispered, hoping to catch the dog's ear without alerting the trespassers that he was aware of their presence.

Andy quieted for a moment, just long enough for Hampton to hear a couple of mumbled voices arguing among themselves. Andy set to howling and barking again.

Hampton eased around the side of the house, working his way along the log wall, then crouching as he reached the corner.

Sensing his presence, Andy growled instead of barking.

Hampton lowered himself to the ground, then pointed his carbine in the direction of the Blunt ranch. "Andy," he whispered, "come here, boy."

The dog approached the corner, blocking Hampton's view for a moment as he stopped, then spun around and growled again.

Someone was trying to slip up on the house!

Hampton could hear the whisper of dry grass being crossed and he knew someone was approaching to plant or throw dynamite. This was how the Gillyards had been assassinated.

Andy's growl grew deeper and Hampton squinted to see the trespasser. Hampton's finger slipped to the trigger.

Then he saw a sudden flare of light.

A match had been struck.

He swung the rifle toward the ball of light. He recognized Cyrus McCurdy, one of Blunt's men, and squeezed off a shot. The match went dark, but by the whine of the bullet Hampton knew he had missed.

"Damnation," cried McCurdy. "Let's get out of here."

"Run, boys, run for it," called a voice Hampton recognized as Lem Blunt's.

Hampton fired again and again, working the carbine lever smoothly, efficiently as he shot at invisible noises. In the darkness he heard the sound of several men running. Then the night exploded with several shots, which plunked into the corner of the cabin.

Andy yelped, then barked, madder than before.

Hampton rolled away from the corner, then scrambled to his feet and darted around the cabin.

Jerking a box of cartridges from his pocket, he reloaded his carbine as fast as he could. He waited for another flash of gunfire. He saw nothing but heard the sound of galloping horses and men cursing.

"Damn you, you yellow sons of bitches," he yelled, shaking his fist at the sounds and the darkness.

He kept his position for a while in case someone had lingered behind to bushwhack him if he turned careless. When he felt confident he was alone, he called for Andy. "Here, boy, come here, Andy."

The dog shuffled toward him, whining as he approached.

Hampton patted the dog on the head and felt his fur sticky with blood. "Good dog," he said, "good dog."

He squatted and picked up the dog in his arms and carried him to the porch and then inside. The dog was listless in his arms and seemed limp when he placed him on the table. He propped his carbine against the wall and lit a lamp; the room glowed a sickly yellow.

Hampton cursed at Andy's bloodied head, but his fingers probing the dog's skull quickly told him Andy had only been creased, just behind his stubby ear.

He grabbed a dipper and plunged it into the water barrel, then retrieved a cup of the precious liquid. He poured it over Andy's head. The water seemed to revive the mongrel and he tried to lick Hampton's fingers. "You'll live," Hampton pronounced, then collapsed into a chair and shook his head. Blunt would be back. He would keep attacking until Hampton was dead.

Exhausted from the strain and the worry, Hampton slumped over on the table to rest for a few minutes. The minutes grew longer, and when Hampton finally awoke at the touch of Andy's tongue licking his face, it was past dawn.

Hampton bolted out of the chair, grabbed his carbine and emerged into the morning light. Starting close to the cabin, he began to scour the perimeter in ever-widening circles, until he found something that made his blood curdle.

A stick of dynamite.

It wasn't quite within throwing distance of the cabin, but it was close enough to have done some damage even if it had fallen short.

Hampton nodded at Andy, who was sniffing at a spot on the ground. "You saved my life last night." Hampton picked up the stick of dynamite, pulled the fuse and blasting cap from it, tossing them aside, then walked over to Andy to see what he had found.

There was a palm-size bloodstain upon the ground. "Winged one of them, didn't I?"

By the time Hampton finished his search, he had found the hulls from where Blunt's men had fired back and the places where they had tied their horses. Hampton figured there were five horses. He hoped there were no more.

Five horses would account for Blunt and his four hands.

More horses would suggest Blunt's daughters had ridden with them. Hampton couldn't stomach the idea that he might have to kill Charlie and Josie.

10

By midmorning Hugh Hampton was tired of the waiting. Sitting at the table chewing on jerky for his meager breakfast, he felt like a steer in a slaughterhouse, waiting for the inevitable. Being the snakes they were, Blunt and his men likely wouldn't attack during the day. They would wait for the cover of darkness, then try to assassinate him.

Hampton cursed in frustration. He had gone to the law and been humiliated and threatened. He had done what was right, what was lawful, without success. Now he must act. This wasn't vigilante justice, but self-defense. A man had a right to defend himself and his property. Maybe Hampton couldn't save his place from the drought, but he could damn sure protect it from Blunt and his evil.

Pushing himself up from the table, he opened a cartridge box and filled every empty loop on his holster. Then he strode into his bedroom, jerking an old army cartridge belt from a nail on the wall and returning to the table to fill it with ammunition. He buckled the cartridge belt, then draped it over his head and right shoulder like a bandolier. Picking up his carbine from the table, he looked for his hat, finding it on the chair in his bedroom where he had tossed it the night before. He snugged the hat tight over his head.

He was almost out the door when he spotted his canteen on a peg. He would need it. He grabbed the container by its leather strap and jerked it from the peg, the water sloshing around inside. He slid the canteen under his arm, unplugged the cork, then lifted the container to his lips and drew deeply on the warm water. The liquid washed away the salty taste of jerky. Retreating to the water barrel, Hampton dropped the canteen inside. It sank in a storm of bubbles that stilled once the canteen filled. Pulling it clear of the barrel, Hampton recorked it, hung it over his shoulders and bounded out the door for the barn, Andy trailing in his wake.

The sky was tinged copper by a fiery, withering sun that baked the land. Even in the shade of the barn, Hampton felt the sun's intense heat. He saddled his chestnut quickly, then secured his canteen and Henry. As he was about to mount, he felt in his pocket the stick of dynamite he had picked up after the aborted raid last night. He removed it and slipped it into his saddlebag with the Gillyard Bible. As Andy ambled into the adjacent stall and lay down, panting from the heat, Hampton led the chestnut out of the barn, then mounted up.

In a moment Andy emerged, his head hanging listlessly from the graze wound he had sustained in the shoot-out.

Hampton shook the reins and aimed his gelding for the creek. Andy padded after him a few steps until Hampton twisted around in the saddle. "Stay, Andy, stay." The mongrel stopped, shook his head gingerly, then ambled lazily toward the porch and his favorite spot of shade.

Hampton swung his horse wide of the direct route to the Blunt house, figuring to reduce the likelihood of a chance encounter with Blunt or his hands. From the lack of sleep, he was initially drowsy, but once he crossed onto Blunt land his taut nerves kept him attentive. Frequently, he twisted around and looked behind him. Though he had seen no sign to support his fears, he had a creeping dread that someone was following him, watching his every move.

"Easy," he said to his gelding, though he knew he was talking more to himself.

This was a fool's expedition, he knew. He should never have gone out alone against Blunt without letting Gibson and the others know. If something happened to him like happened to Simon Levine, no one would ever know. Hampton laughed bitterly. What difference did that make? The law wouldn't do a damn thing about it anyway.

Hampton cursed his edginess as he came within a mile of the Blunt ranch quarters. Behind a low hill that blocked his approach, Hampton hobbled and tied his chestnut in a grove of mesquite trees. Untying his canteen, he hung it over his head and shoulder, then pulled his Henry from its scabbard and started marching. He figured he could get within a quarter of a mile of the place easily, but he needed to be closer if he were to have a legitimate chance at picking off Lemuel Blunt.

He moved quickly, stealthily toward the Blunt place, skirting the edge of the hill, then advancing from tree to tree, hiding occasionally behind a clump of prickly pear. At a half-mile, the ranch house came into view. He squatted down in the shade of a mesquite tree and studied the place. Hampton cursed when he saw that the corrals were empty of all but three horses. That likely meant Blunt was away. "Damn him," Hampton said in frustration.

A wisp of smoke trailed out of the stovepipe, but otherwise the place seemed abandoned. He slipped forward, seeking to close the gap between himself and the ranch buildings. He made it to within a quarter of a mile before the cover thinned. He slid to the ground in the shade of a live oak and waited, studying the terrain for a location that might offer a better shot. Blunt had picked his home site well, for this was about as close as Hampton could get and still have cover.

The heat was stifling as Hampton waited and watched. His shirt was soon soaked with perspiration and he unbuttoned the bib front, hoping that it might bring a bit of relief. Nothing helped, not even the swig of water he took from the canteen.

Gradually, the heat sapped his energy, until he was as lethargic as the breeze. He stared through the shimmering heat, but did not see. Then a noise caught his ear and he shook his head clear of the muddle and blinked his eyes. It had sounded like a muffled scream. He tensed and lifted the carbine to his chest, ready to react.

Then he saw the door of the bunkhouse fly open and a woman run out. From the distance, Hampton could not tell if it was Josie or Charlie, just that it was one of them and she was naked, holding her clothes balled up in front of her as she ran toward the main house. He watched her naked bronze form, her long black hair trailing behind her as she escaped. In a moment she was in the house, slamming the door behind her.

As Hampton glanced back at the bunkhouse, he saw Ivey Yates slip outside. Yates wore a shirt that dropped below his waist, but no britches. Hampton gritted his teeth. One of Blunt's daughters had just been raped. Hampton lifted his rifle and drew a bead on Yates. His finger quivered against the trigger, then fell away.

Blunt must die first. He lowered the rifle, his stomach knotting in disgust. Especially galling was County Attorney Royce Dugan's threat to prosecute Hampton on rape charges while so many other men were abusing the two sisters.

Yates stretched, then strolled to the nearby outhouse. In a few minutes he returned to the bunkhouse, disappearing inside for a bit, then emerging again in his work clothes. Yates strode to the corral, roped and saddled a horse. He mounted and rode away, passing beneath the rise and near the clump of rocks where Hampton and Let Gibson had found the cache of whiskey. Hampton hoped Yates wasn't carrying dynamite to blow up his place in his absence.

Shortly, Hampton saw one of the women emerge from the house to draw a bucket of water from the cistern. Hampton could not identify her from this distance, but she was fully dressed. Once she'd collected water she disappeared back inside.

Except for that brief moment, Hampton saw no more activity. The minutes dragged by like hours and Hampton's stomach growled for food. The canteen water quenched his thirst but not his hunger. By midafternoon, he knew he must start back home.

Let Gibson was supposed to pull a watch this evening, and Hampton feared Gibson might confuse him with one of Blunt's men. Gibson could be unpredictable, especially if he had had a drink, though Hampton hoped his threat had scared sobriety into Gibson for a while. Gradually, Hampton retreated, ever careful to use each tree, bush and clump of cactus to screen his withdrawal. As he made his way back to his gelding, he was troubled by doubts about how Charlie and Josie stood with their father and his men. From what he had seen, he could not see how either could tolerate the treatment, except out of fear, but that was just speculation.

At a half-mile distance from the ranch buildings, Hampton relaxed. He was out of sight of the place, so he swigged water from his canteen. He took a mouthful and held it within his cheeks, relishing the moisture upon his parched tongue. Then he took off his hat and poured a cup more inside. He threw his hat on top of his head, grateful for the momentary coolness as the water trickled through his hair and down his face.

When he reached his chestnut, Hampton took off his hat and emptied the rest of the canteen into the crown. He held the hat up to the chestnut's mouth and the horse drank the water greedily.

"Sorry I had to leave you tied up in this heat, old boy, but it wasn't any more comfortable for me out there."

Returning the hat to his head, Hampton tied the canteen in place, then tucked the carbine into his saddle holster. After untying the horse, Hampton mounted up and started the gelding on a wide arc back toward his cabin.

He had ridden no more than half an hour

when he caught a glimpse of a distant rider. Hampton thought he recognized Gibson, but hid behind a pair of live oaks just to be certain. Gibson did not spot Hampton until he rode out from behind the two trees, waving his hat over his head.

Gibson flinched and went for his gun before he realized who it was. He relaxed and slapped his reins against his stallion's neck. The powerful animal lunged forward and was quickly upon Hampton.

"You scared the devil out of me, Hugh," Gibson said, licking the perspiration from his lips.

"Didn't mean to, Let."

"Anyway, I thought it was my evening to keep an eye on the Blunt place."

"It is, Let," Hampton acknowledged, "but they tried to blow up my place last night."

"Damn them to hell," Gibson cursed.

"I figured I might be able to ambush Blunt myself and put an end to all this meanness. If we don't end it soon, they're gonna kill us like the Gillyards."

"Any activity at the Blunt place?"

Hampton sighed. "No sign of Blunt. Just saw one of the girls and Ivey Yates, who rode off toward my place a couple hours ago. The rest of the horses are gone, so I reckon Blunt and his hands are up to some mischief somewhere. Did Johnny Walls spot anything unusual yesterday evening?"

"Maybe," Gibson answered. "After supper he said Blunt made a ride around the place, sticking to the rise and inspecting things, spending a little more time down the rise in the direction of your place."

Hampton shook his head. "I heard his voice last night and saw Cyrus McCurdy when he tried to light a fuse."

"Did they do any damage?"

"Not this time. I scared them off before they could explode any dynamite, but they'll be back. You and I know it."

Gibson nodded. "Until we're dead."

"Keep a good eye on the Blunt place, but stay out of sight."

Gibson patted the field glasses hanging from his neck. "These should help."

"And Let, if it's safe, you get away from here as soon as you can. I don't like Matilda being alone with this trouble working."

"If they harm that woman, I'll kill them all," Gibson growled.

Hampton pointed behind him. "Stand your watch and good luck. Tomorrow swap off the glasses with Spud Davis and make sure he knows of anything in particular to look for."

"Good as done," Gibson said, rattling the

reins and starting his horse toward the Blunt place.

Hampton watched him disappear among the mesquite, then continued his journey back toward home. He watched the distant skies, half expecting to see a funnel of smoke arising from his place. In his absence, the Blunt hands could have fired his cabin and burned it to the ground. Of course, as dry as it was, they might risk burning the whole county down, but what did they care?

As he topped the last rise to his place, Hampton reined up and studied the cabin, barn and corral. Nothing seemed amiss with the buildings. Next, Hampton studied the land and trees, looking for potential assassins. Seeing nothing suspicious, he eased his chestnut forward and aimed him for the barn.

As he reached the barn door, he saw Andy curled up in the shade under the porch. The dog made no move to greet him and Hampton attributed his listlessness to the heat and the wound he sustained in the attack.

After tending his horse, Hampton started for the house, carrying the carbine in one hand and the canteen in another. "Here, Andy, come here, boy," he yelled.

The dog did not move.

"Andy," Hampton yelled as he bolted for

the animal.

As he reached the porch, he saw what he had feared. Andy had been shot.

Hampton cursed, knowing that Blunt's men would be back tonight to kill him like they had killed his dog.

11

Hugh Hampton could have used a little more time before dusk set in. He had buried Andy in a shallow grave, then carried stones from the virtually dry creek bed and piled them over his dog so the coyotes would not uncover him. He had greased and oiled his carbine as he figured his strategy.

His cabin had no window facing the creek, the side the attack would come from, so Hampton knew he must abandon it. He could hide in the open and await his attackers. He would have a clear view of the area, but it increased the chances he might be spotted. Or, he could hide in the barn and wait it out. The barn might be a target, but not if Blunt thought him asleep in the cabin. Too, in the barn Hampton would be near his saddled horse in case he needed to make a dash for safety. A saddled horse outside the cabin would look too suspicious.

He took a canvas bag from his bedroom

and stuffed a change of clothes inside, then shoved in his three remaining cartons of ammunition to augment the bullets in his two gun belts. He took two tins of peaches from a wall shelf and added them to the war bag, then filled his canteen from the dwindling water barrel.

As darkness began to envelop the land, he poured the coal oil from his kitchen lamp into a tin, leaving but half a cupful in the lamp. He lit the lamp and adjusted the flame low, then exited the cabin with the war bag, canteen and his carbine. In the barn, he saddled his chestnut hurriedly, tying the war bag over the saddlebags and hanging the canteen over the saddle horn.

Still carrying his carbine, he retreated back to the cabin, the kitchen window glowing softly from the low-burning lamp. Were anyone watching, Hampton hoped the spy would think he had merely been checking his horse and shutting up the barn.

Hampton entered the house and started a fire in the stove, figuring the smell of burning wood on a hot night might lead any enemy to think he was cooking his supper. His tricks with the lamp and the stove might be worthless if Blunt waited until after midnight to attack, but Hampton knew he had to stay busy to keep his nerves from snapping.

He did not know how long the lamp would burn before it consumed the kerosene, but he hoped long enough to give the impression that he had blown out the lamp and retired. Hampton figured he had done about as much as he could, until a terrible thought hit him. What if the same person who had killed Andy had buried dynamite around the house?

Hampton had failed to inspect the exterior and now it was dark. It would be impossible to check without a lamp, and any light would only make Hampton a good target for anyone who might be out there. He could check in the morning, but not now. Hampton clanged a skillet against the cast-iron stove, trying to further his deceit. Then, with carbine in his hand, he slipped into his bedroom and closed the door behind him so the lamplight did not shine inside. He took a dark wool blanket from the end of his bed and draped it Indian style around himself to help disguise his movement when he went to the barn.

Then he stood by the open window in the side wall, listening for suspicious noises. He planned to leave by the window so anyone watching the door might not know of his escape. Hearing nothing out of the ordinary, he slid his left leg out, then worked his torso through the window, dragging his right leg behind him. Tugging the blanket over his hat and head with his free hand, he crouched and circled wide of the house to miss the rectangle of lamplight that seeped from the kitchen window. He made it quickly and easily to the barn, slipping inside.

The chestnut stamped and blew nervously. Pulling the blanket from over his shoulders, Hampton patted the gelding to calm him, then folded the blanket and tied it behind the saddle. When the horse quit stamping, Hampton considered his options.

The barn had a sloped roof, and beneath the high side Hampton had built a loft that ran the length of the twenty-foot structure. He stored feed there, as well as some of his tools. At both ends of the loft he had made drop doors so he could reach the loft from the outside. Hampton climbed up the inside ladder and crawled to the front of the loft, where he released the latch and slowly pushed the hinged door open.

Lying down in front of the opening, he studied the cabin and the surroundings as best he could in the dark. Nothing seemed amiss, but the wait had just begun. It was boring, tedious duty staring into the darkness, waiting for something he expected but could not be certain was actually coming. He worried that Blunt's men had already planted dynamite around the house and had only to come back and light the fuse to do their dirty work.

That thought worried him, but another really scared him. What if they had planted dynamite around the barn as well? Hampton clenched his teeth, mad at himself for not checking either building while it was still light. The night was still, which meant sound would carry far; it also meant the barn was suffocatingly hot without a breeze.

Hampton had to fight off sleep. The oppressive heat and the exhaustion from the previous night's sparse rest weighed heavily on his eyelids, which drooped in spite of his best effort to keep them open. He managed to stay awake past midnight, if not totally alert. Then, despite his efforts, he dozed off, waking periodically, then falling into a deep sleep.

When something finally stirred him, it took him a moment to collect his senses. He heard noises, the low calls of plotting men. Then he heard a soft, sputtering hiss.

Shaking his head of the sleep, he lifted his eyes in time to see a trail of flame making its way toward his cabin. He caught his impulse to yell. It was too late to do anything, and yelling would only give away his position. He swung his Henry around, looking for anyone in the dark, but he saw nothing.

Except the moving, sputtering flame!

All Hampton thought about was the hours of hard work he had put into building the modest cabin.

The flame neared the building.

Damn Lemuel Blunt, he thought.

Then the flame disappeared for a moment.

Hampton smiled. Had the fuse burned itself out?

Then the night exploded with noise and light.

Hampton cried out at the noise, but his shout was lost in the explosion.

The landscape flamed with an instant light, and for a moment Hampton thought he saw Lem Blunt standing in the distance with two other men. Then the flame became blinding and Hampton shut his eyes.

The noise rolled over him, then the heat from the explosion. The gates of hell could be no worse than this. Hampton sucked in his breath and the very air seemed to scorch the inside of his lungs.

He gasped, then opened his eyes and saw

flaming debris shooting skyward and showering down upon the earth. There was a pounding noise in the air and a scream of terror. Beyond the giant flame that had been his home he saw the shapes of Blunt and his men, quivering like demons from hell in the heat. Hampton lifted his carbine, aiming to send Blunt to hell where he belonged. But the fire was so intense that he couldn't hold his eyes open.

Hampton retreated deeper into the barn and for the first time realized the pounding on the wall was his terrified chestnut, kicking at his stall and trying to get free. Then Hampton began to smell smoke and rolled over to the edge of the loft.

The barn had taken blaze at the front corner and the hay on the floor was smoldering. He glanced out the loft door a final time, wishing for a chance to kill Blunt, but he had lost the rancher in the darkness somewhere beyond the flames.

Hampton scrambled to the ladder, losing his grip on his carbine, then backtracking to get it. He clenched his fingers around it and crawled to the ladder, then clambered down it, dropping the carbine at his feet. He cursed as he bent and retrieved it. The fire was spreading quickly through the dry hay and flames were licking at the low corner of the barn. Behind him the chestnut whinnied and kicked in terror.

The carbine firmly gripped in his left hand, he jumped at the fire and stomped at it with his boots. The smoke was rising, stinging his eyes and blinding him. The dry wood of the wall before him was flecked with yellow tongues of flame that lapped toward the door, Hampton's only route of escape except a side door that emptied into the corral. If he escaped out the side, Hampton knew he might be shot in the corral before he could open the gate. The front door was his only escape, but he had to act quickly because the chestnut was terrified, jumping, thrashing and kicking.

Hampton spun around and ran to the chestnut, stripping the blanket from behind the saddle and flinging it at the horse's head, once, twice, three times before covering the gelding's eyes. Hampton grabbed the gelding's reins, wrapping them tightly around his right hand and somehow managing to mount the frightened animal without dropping his carbine. The ceiling was low under the loft and the chestnut bucked, driving Hampton's head into a rafter. Hampton cried out, then gritted his teeth against the pain and jerked the reins savagely, momentarily subduing the horse. He backed the animal out of the stall, then leaned forward and shoved his carbine in its scabbard. The horse began to bounce and buck. Hampton jerked the reins as hard as he could for control. Acrid smoke filled the barn and the front wall — and the door to safety — was a curtain of flame.

Hampton leaned forward in the saddle, holding the reins as near the bit as he could reach. He kicked the gelding with his boot heels, then slapped the chestnut's neck and screamed at the top of his seared lungs. Its head still covered with the woolen blanket, the horse bolted forward, straight for the door. Hampton held on for his life, leaning as low as he could so the top of the door frame didn't knock him out of the saddle. He prayed for surefootedness from the gelding when it hit the door.

All of a sudden the curtain of flame engulfed him as the gelding banged the door at full stride. Hampton felt the flames lick his skin. He caught a sharp breath at the momentary pain and seemed to suck the flame into his lungs. The horse stumbled as the door swung around on its hinges.

The woolen blanket covering the gelding's head snagged on the door and flew free as the chestnut plunged toward the burning cabin. Hampton jerked the reins and steered the gelding away from both flames.

Hampton heard shouts and shots behind him. He clung low to the terrified chestnut's neck in the dash for safety. The horse lunged ahead with a powerful stride that soon carried Hampton beyond gunshot range. Gradually, he straightened in the saddle and looked over his shoulder at the voracious flames consuming years of past work and future dreams. He cursed at the darkness and at the figures he could see dancing on the perimeter of the fire like demons.

Slowly, he pulled back on the reins, letting the gelding slow gradually. The chestnut eased into a trot, then into a nervous walk, tossing and shaking its head.

Hampton turned his horse off the trail and angled him up a hill, where he stopped and watched the barn collapse under the flames. He waited and listened for the sound of horses that might be bringing Blunt and his men after him. After the hellish flame he had just ridden through, the heat of the night seemed cool by comparison.

Beyond the remains of his flaming cabin, the explosion had spread debris all around his place and fire had jumped the creek. A low fire was marching over the grass toward Blunt's ranch.

Hampton coughed some of the smoke

from his lungs and spat at the ground. Maybe the fire would destroy Blunt and his land. Hampton shook his head. No, he didn't want that. He wanted to kill Blunt himself.

Certain that Blunt's men were more concerned with stopping the grassfire than with finding him, Hampton unhooked the canteen from his saddle and lapped at the water, relishing its cool wetness in his dry mouth.

He turned his horse toward the Gibsons' place, hoping no misfortune had befallen Let and Matilda. He rode slowly, trying to reserve what strength the gelding still possessed in case he needed it for later. Too, he didn't want to create any noise that might attract undue attention, should other people be out in the night.

When he came within a half-mile of the Gibson place, he stopped and studied the terrain. Everything was dark, the crescent moon shedding barely enough light for him to make out the darkened stone house. He rode slowly, and as he came within a hundred yards of the place, he began to yell.

"Let, Matilda. It's Hugh Hampton. I'm coming in," he shouted. "Don't shoot. You hear?"

Nothing but silence answered.

Hampton shouted a repeat warning. "Hello the house!"

Finally the silence was broken by a voice Hampton recognized as Let's. "Come again."

Hampton cupped his hands at his mouth and answered. "It's Hugh Hampton. I'm coming in. Don't shoot."

There was a pause. "It don't sound like Hugh Hampton."

As much smoke as he had swallowed, maybe his voice didn't sound normal.

"How do I know it's Hugh?" Let called back.

"Don't shoot, Let," Hampton yelled through cupped hands. "I want some more of Matilda's pecan pie."

"Come on in, Hugh," answered Let. "We'll light a lamp for you."

Hampton lowered his hands from his face, shaking his head. He didn't know if he wanted to see another flame again, even in a lamp.

Soon a pale glow appeared through a front window, then the whole parlor lit up. Let Gibson emerged on the porch, cradling a rifle in his arms. Behind him, Matilda in her nightgown stood squarely in the door, her silhouette as menacing as the shotgun she carried.

"What the hell brings you out, Hugh?" called Let.

Without answering, Hampton dismounted at the front steps and tied his horse, then strode onto the porch into the murky light.

"My God, Hugh, what happened?" cried Matilda.

"Blunt, wasn't it?" Gibson asked.

Hampton nodded. "They came for me."

Matilda propped her shotgun up against the stone wall and barged past Gibson to Hampton.

"Don't trample me, woman," Gibson scowled.

"Hush, Let, he's hurt."

Matilda took him by the arm and led him inside.

Gibson trailed them, shaking his head. "Looks like they tried to roast you, Hugh."

Matilda steered Hampton to a chair by the kitchen table.

"They blew up my cabin, just like they did the Gillyards'."

"You sure it wasn't another cyclone and lightning?" Gibson asked sarcastically.

"Hush, Let, and give the man a chance to tell his story. How'd you survive the explosion?"

Hampton turned to Gibson. "After I left you on the Blunt place, I returned home to

151

find Andy shot. I knew they would be coming back tonight. Andy's the only thing that saved me last night.

"I hid out in the barn waiting, but it was late and I fell asleep before they arrived. When I woke up, they'd already lit the fuse. I made out Blunt, Cyrus McCurdy and Ivey Yates for sure. There was another one or two with them."

"What about those daughters of Blunt's?" asked Matilda. "Were they there?"

Hampton shook his head. "Not that I saw. Anyway, the barn caught on fire and I had to make a run for it. The whole place burned down."

"Bastards," Gibson growled. "Did they chase you?"

"Nope. Best I could tell, the explosion caught a grassfire that was moving toward the Blunt place."

Matilda crossed the room to a bucket and dipped a rag in the water. She returned and began to dab at the grit that had dried with the sweat on his face. His skin was sensitive in places and he flinched at the touch. "You're lucky you weren't burned worse. It's red as a sunburn in places."

Hampton felt the pain at her touch, but even more he felt anger raging out of control within him. He wanted Blunt and

152

would get him.

"Come light, I'll need to wash your clothes," she said, "to get the dirt out."

"Thanks, Matilda." Hampton turned to Gibson. "What did you see on your watch tonight?"

"Nothing out of the ordinary, other than old man Blunt made a ride around the place an hour or so before dark. Johnny Walls saw the same thing. Don't know if it's habit or not, but that's what we've seen the first two days. A couple more days and we'll know for sure."

Hampton shook his head. "We can't afford two more days; by then there may not be any of us."

Gibson paced back and forth across the kitchen, scratching his chin as he moved. "You remember when we followed the tracks from the Gillyard place?"

"Yeah." Hampton nodded.

"We found a couple bottles of liquor in that rock pile."

"I remember it."

"Think that could be Blunt's whiskey?"

Hampton grinned. "I bet it is. He lets his men manhandle his daughters while he goes out for a drink."

Gibson slapped his thigh. "I think all we've got to do is go out there and poison his whiskey."

Hampton's grin disappeared. "No, sir."

Gibson appeared shocked. "Why not?"

"I don't want to poison him. I want to watch him die," Hampton said, his voice hard as his words. He stared through Gibson, his gaze like granite. "And I intend to kill him before nightfall."

12

Grim-faced, they approached Johnny Walls's cabin, Hugh Hampton and Let Gibson riding side by side. Hampton shouted their approach.

Walls emerged shirtless and hatless. He carried his Winchester at his side. Behind him, his new wife stood in the door, nervously peeking outside.

Hampton was in no mood for long explanations. "We're killing him tonight. He blew up my cabin, burned my barn last night. We wait any longer, it could be you and your wife." Hampton tipped his hat in acknowledgment of the new Mrs. Walls.

She raised her hand to her throat, her eyes widening with fear.

"You in or out, Johnny?" asked Gibson.

"No," cried his wife. "What about the law? Can't the law handle this?"

Johnny walked over to his wife and put his arm around her shoulder, drawing her to him. "It'll be okay."

"Not if you get hurt." Her eyes filled with tears.

"I can get killed just tending my chores, as long as Lem Blunt's loose." He drew her tighter to him.

Hampton lifted his hat and nodded at the woman. "No offense, ma'am, but I need an answer from your husband. You going to the dance or not, Johnny?"

Pursing his lips, Walls nodded.

His wife started crying.

"Where you headed?" Johnny asked.

"Over to Spud's place next, then to Winfrey's."

"Go on," he said, "and I'll catch up with you."

Hampton lowered his hat. "Sorry, ma'am, and I'll do everything I can to see your husband returns safe and sound." He turned his chestnut toward Spud Davis's ranch.

Gibson rode beside Hampton, neither man speaking. What was there to say? The land needed rain. The days were hotter than hell on a griddle. Folks' livestock were dying. The law was rigged in Brown County. And, Lemuel Blunt was a mean bastard. That had all been said before. Now, though, Hampton planned on giving the residents of Brown County one less problem to worry about.

Halfway to Davis's place, Hampton heard the sound of a galloping horse behind him. He twisted in his saddle to see Johnny Walls approaching. Walls eased off on his bay mare and apologized as he came within talking distance.

"My wife didn't mean nothing, Hugh."

"It's no matter," Hampton answered. "I'm in no mood for discussing the issue. I lost everything last night except what dry grass didn't burn and what cattle haven't died already."

Gibson guided his stallion beside Walls's mare and slapped Johnny on the shoulder. "I'm glad to see you finished getting dressed, Johnny. Of course, knowing you needed extra time with the pretty little woman, I wouldn't have been surprised you showing up without your pants."

Hampton felt a grin work across his face. Gibson had a way of either making a situation tolerable or letting it get completely out of hand. By the flush in Walls's cheek, Hampton knew Gibson had pegged the situation just right.

"Been years since I had a pretty little woman," Gibson continued.

Walls protested. "What about Matilda?"

"Hell, Johnny, ain't you seen her? She's a pretty big woman, a Texas-sized woman if I ever saw one."

They all managed a laugh, then continued in silence toward Spud Davis's place. They caught Davis mounted on horseback in a pasture, holding a coil of rope and driving a dozen steers toward what was left of Pecan Creek. When he saw riders, Davis jerked his carbine from his scabbard before he recognized them. He pulled off his hat and waved them on in. Hampton's gelding led the procession at a trot.

"A man can't be too careful," he explained, shoving his carbine back in place. "Bad news?"

Hampton nodded. "They blew up my cabin last night, burned my barn. We intend to get him tonight. Are you with us?"

"It's my night to watch." He held up the coil of rope. "I suspect Blunt would look good at the end of this." He turned his horse in with the others and whistled at the cattle. They jumped into a lope and scattered like quail. "I've seen fence posts with more meat on them."

"At least you've still got a cabin," Hampton said bitterly.

After a moment of quiet, Gibson spoke. "Time's a wasting and we've still got to notify Frank Winfrey."

The four men turned their horses toward Winfrey's place, Hampton and Gibson riding side by side in the lead, Davis and Walls following. Hampton said nothing, just stared straight down the trail, ever vigilant of the dangers that might be lurking ahead. The trip from Davis's took an hour.

As the four men rounded the pecan trees that followed a curve along the virtually dry creek bed, Hampton was the first to see the open gate of the corral. Hampton grabbed his carbine; his sudden movement startled the others and they reached for their weapons. Hampton sniffed at the air.

"What's the matter?" called Davis.

Hampton pointed with the barrel of his gun at the corral. "Winfrey wouldn't leave his gate open like that. He's had visitors . . . and something's dead."

The riders held their positions a moment, surveying the surroundings, looking for any clue that might help them find Winfrey or explain his absence.

"Frank Winfrey," Hampton shouted, "it's Hugh Hampton and your neighbors. Where are you? We're here to help."

Receiving no answer, Hampton led the three men toward the small barn. As he rode past the barn, Hampton held up his hand

and pointed to a dead horse sprawled upon the ground, its body swollen from the heat and its left legs pointed stiffly to the sky.

"That ain't Winfrey's horse," Gibson offered, pulling his kerchief up over his nose.

Hampton aimed his chestnut for the yellow dun, studying its exposed hip. "Look at the brand."

Gibson cursed. "The Lazy B."

"Lem Blunt's brand," sighed Johnny Walls, holding his hand over his nose.

"Damn shame Frank didn't get Blunt," Spud Davis said as he tied his kerchief around his face.

Hampton turned his chestnut away from the horse and toward the cabin. As the chestnut neared the far end of the cabin, he balked, refusing to go further until Hampton kicked him in the flank. The horse advanced reluctantly. Hampton knew what he would find there — Frank Winfrey.

The rancher was splayed upon the ground, his blood splattered against the house timbers, his torso riddled with bullets. Like the horse, his body was bloated. Hampton turned his head and pulled his kerchief over his nose. "Here's his body," Hampton called as Gibson rode up beside him.

"Damn to hell the bastards that did this," Gibson cried out, then spat at the ground.

Walls and Davis joined Hampton and Gibson. For a moment, the four men said nothing to one another, staring at the body and wondering why fate had picked Winfrey to die rather than one of them.

Finally, Walls climbed out of the saddle and stomped the ground. "Let's get him buried, then let's get Lem Blunt."

Hampton rode around the cabin, looking for other dangers. After circling the cabin, he saw Gibson emerging from the barn with a shovel and a pick. Hampton pointed to the creek. "The ground's likely softer there. Start digging his grave and we'll swap out. One of us needs to stay mounted and alert in case they come back to burn the horse or cut off the brand."

Gibson scowled. "Only a fool wouldn't destroy the brand."

"A fool," said Hampton, "or a man who's friends with the sheriff and the county attorney."

"I'll start digging," Gibson volunteered, "and Hugh, you keep watch for a spell." He turned to Walls and Davis. "Gather what rocks you can from the creek bed to cover the grave."

The men went about their business, swapping off periodically. When the grave was sufficiently deep, all four approached the body, each grabbing an arm or a leg and toting the body like a sack of potatoes to the grave. They laid him in the ground folding his stiff arms as best they could across his chest, then began to cover him quickly with dirt to kill the stench. After filling the grave, they mounded it over with rocks, the only monument Frank Winfrey would have for a life lived honestly and ended unfairly.

After Walls stacked the last rock atop the gravel each man removed his hat and waited for someone else to say something. Hampton looked around and shrugged. He felt humbled in the presence of death, especially the death of a friend. After a moment of eloquent silence, Hampton pulled his hat back on.

"There's work to be done, boys." Hampton led the others back to their horses. They mounted silently and turned toward the Lazy B.

Once they crossed onto Blunt lands, they pulled their carbines and continued their determined march, riding four abreast beneath a sun that blazed hot, but not nearly as hot as their anger.

By midafternoon, they had ridden to within two miles of the ranch house. Hampton spoke, "I want to hang the son of a bitch if we can catch him. If we can't catch him, then we'll shoot him."

Davis scratched his head. "How we gonna get close enough to do either without alerting him and his men?"

"The last two nights after supper," replied Hampton, "Blunt's made a circle around the place, spending a little time at a rock pile just beneath the rise that leads up to his place."

"Yeah," interjected Gibson, "Hugh and I found a couple liquor bottles there we think belongs to him. He likes to take a little nip every night after supper and is too stingy to share good whiskey with his men."

"What if he doesn't come out tonight?" Walls asked.

Hampton looked Walls straight in the eye. "Then you better hope your wife knows how to defend herself."

Walls swallowed hard.

Gibson broke in. "It's a risk, boys, but it's better than letting them pick us off one by one like they did Frank."

"Anybody that wants to back out can do so now," Hampton said, looking from face to face, trying to gauge each man's resolve. "No questions asked, no hard feelings, but now's the time to quit. Can't afford for anyone to have second thoughts once the ball starts rolling. Are you all in?"

"To the bitter end," Gibson answered instantly.

"For Frank," said Davis.

Walls looked from man to man and answered each with a determined nod. "What's the plan, Hugh?"

"How we position ourselves depends on what you two observed the last two nights. When Blunt made his round, which way did he go, Johnny?"

"He moved south, then circled around to the rock pile, lingered there, then moved on," Walls replied.

Gibson nodded. "Same when I saw him. He rode around and approached the rocks below the rise where they couldn't see him from the place."

"Are there enough trees for cover near the rocks?" Hampton asked.

"Patchy," Gibson said. "Decent cover for one man, no more."

Hampton nodded. "I figure I'm the best shot. I'll take position in the rocks. If he follows habit, he should be in the rocks fishing out his liquor before he knows I'm there. I should be able to get the drop on him. Let, I want you flat on your belly among the trees. If he tries to escape, open fire. Shoot his horse from under him if that's what it takes; just don't let him get away."

Hampton looked from Walls to Davis, gauging each man. With his new wife at home, Walls had seemed the more reluctant of the two to get drawn into this crime. "Johnny, we've got to keep the horses hidden or the whole thing won't work. I want to leave you about a half mile below the rise. Hobble the horses and hide them among the trees. If we capture him, one of us'll ride his horse to fetch you and the mounts. If things go wrong, Johnny, you come running with our horses at the first gunshot."

Walls nodded.

"But be on the lookout," Hampton admonished him. "We don't know whether the Blunt hands are on the ranch or riding back. Climb a tree and don't let them slip up behind you. If we lose our horses, we're as good as dead."

Hampton pointed at the leather case holding the field glasses on Gibson's saddle and turned to Davis. "You find a position about fifty yards down from Gibson where the sun's at your back so there's no reflection off the lenses. Keep an eye on the place and if you notice anything unusual, signal Gibson so he can alert me."

Hampton looked from man to man. "Does everybody understand what they're to do?"

They all nodded.

"Johnny, you're clear on bringing the horses at the first sound of gunfire?" Hampton asked again.

"It'll take me a minute to get the hobbles off; you sure you want them hobbled?"

"Positive. A minute or two of lost time won't be as bad as risking one of them getting away. String reins like a line of pack-horses so you pull them all when you come."

Hampton was satisfied Walls understood his assignment, but was surprised by Gibson's perplexed gaze.

Gibson stroked his chin, then scratched his ear. "What if his men charge us?"

"We make a stand and defend ourselves!"

"What if his girls ride with them?" Gibson continued. "You know they are good with guns."

Hampton shrugged. "We'll do what we have to do."

"But killing women, Hugh?" Gibson shook his head. "It ain't in my constitution."

"Nor mine, Let, but don't think the Blunt hands wouldn't kill yours or Johnny's wives as brutally as they murdered Frank."

Walls interrupted their discussion. "We can talk it to death or we can start the dance. I'm for dancing, not debating."

Hampton tossed Walls a hard gaze that broke into a slight grin. He liked Walls's grit in standing up to his ranching elders. The remark restored Hampton's faith in Walls's ability to react appropriately when the action started.

Hampton rattled his reins and his horse moved ahead, the other men stringing out behind him. They rode to the base of the rise, then halted out of sight of the Blunt ranch house. Hampton dismounted and crawled to the rock pile. He removed his hat as he lifted his head between two rocks for an inspection of the place. Smoke poured from the stovepipe, and two saddled horses pranced about the corral.

Hampton retreated to the others. "The men must be away." He jerked his carbine from the scabbard and grabbed his canteen. "Let's take our positions so Johnny can hide the horses." Hampton tied his reins to Walls's saddle.

Gibson and Davis slid from their horses, grabbing their canteens and carbines as well. Gibson tossed Davis the case with the field glasses, then tied the reins to Hampton's saddle as Davis tied his to Gibson's. Hampton watched Walls ride off with the horses to conceal them in a clump of brush and live oaks.

Then Hampton scurried for the rocks. The dance had begun.

13

The wait was long and hot among the rocks, made only slightly better by the scattered clouds that occasionally blocked out the sun. His hat by his side, Hampton periodically peeked between the rocks for a view of the place. A couple times he had seen Blunt's daughters make trips to the cistern or to the barn.

A couple hours before sundown, Hampton saw Blunt lead his men in from the north. At this distance Hampton couldn't tell for sure, but he thought one of the hands was riding Frank Winfrey's horse. Hampton looked toward the patch of nearby trees and saw Gibson acknowledge with a nod that he had seen the men's arrival.

Hampton heard a shout he could not make out, then saw Josie emerge from the house. A couple of the hands jumped from their horses and swatted at her behind as she passed on the way to the cistern for more water. Even at this distance, Hampton could make out the men's leering laughs. How could a man allow that to happen to his own daughters, his own flesh and blood? But then how could a man murder Simon Levine or Frank Winfrey or the Gillyard brothers, all decent, law-abiding men? The thought of Lem Blunt's evil soured his blood.

Hampton saw Josie fill a bucket of water and leave it on the porch as she went back inside the house. The men rolled up their sleeves and threw off their hats, then crowded around the bucket, washing their hands and drenching their faces. One by one they went inside, most likely to eat. Hampton judged the sky, figuring they had ninety minutes or less before darkness set in. He hoped Lem Blunt had a hankering for whiskey. The minutes dripped by like molasses before one of the men reappeared on the porch. Shortly, another one came out, his arm around Charlie, dragging her with him. Hampton gritted his teeth.

Blunt finally emerged and built himself a smoke while he watched one of the hands aggravate Charlie. "Come on, you bastard," Hampton said to himself, "keep your date with the devil." Blunt took his time smoking, then stretched and yawned before ambling to his horse.

Hampton caught his breath as he watched.

Blunt stepped into the stirrup, then pulled himself into the saddle. He made some circular motion with his hand, then rode away, just as Walls and Gibson had described.

Hampton ducked behind the rock and glanced at Gibson, who nodded with a big grin. So far it was working just as they had planned. Hampton could hear his heart pounding from the anticipation. It was a bad thing to want to kill a man — unless the man needed killing. Hampton wanted to watch Blunt hang. That was the death Blunt deserved.

Hampton squirmed deeper into the rocks to make sure he would not be seen as Blunt approached. He held the carbine across his waist, his thumb upon the hammer, his index finger upon the trigger.

It seemed forever before he heard the hooves of Blunt's horse nearing. At first Hampton thought someone was accompanying Blunt because he heard voices, then he realized Blunt was singing. Hampton recognized the words and gritted his teeth at the blasphemy. Blunt was singing "Amazing Grace," at least part of it. He didn't seem to know all the words. Had he been drinking already?

"Amazing grace," he bellowed, "how great the sound . . ."

Hampton felt the anger exploding within himself like the dynamite that had blown up his cabin. He wanted to jump up and shoot Blunt in that instant, but he did not know exactly where he was.

". . . that saved a wretch like me . . ."

Hampton wondered where Blunt had ever learned the lyrics. If he had been in a church, he hadn't learned much else for the good.

". . . I once was lost . . ."

He was drawing nearer. Hampton could almost feel his evil presence.

". . . but now am found . . ."

Hampton's finger began to tighten against the trigger. He was ready to kill him.

Now the lyrics failed Blunt and he started over. "Amazing grace, how great the sound . . ."

Then Hampton heard a sudden buzzing and the whinny of Blunt's horse.

Blunt cursed. "Son of a bitch."

The stillness was shattered by one gunshot, then a second.

Hampton lifted his head in time to see Gibson motioning for him to stay low. Something had gone wrong, but what?

Hampton ducked back again and cursed to himself. The shots would send Johnny Walls charging in with the horses. The plan was falling apart.

Before Hampton could react, he heard galloping hoofbeats and saw Blunt ride by. He lifted his head in time to see Blunt stop atop the rise and wave his hat over his head.

"Killed a rattlesnake," he yelled toward the house, then turned his horse around.

Hampton ducked behind the rock as Blunt rode back by and halted his horse just beyond the rock pile.

Slowly, Hampton lifted his head and his carbine.

He saw Blunt's back just as he started lifting his leg over the saddle. Then in the distance, Hampton heard the thunder of Walls riding in with the horses.

"What the hell!" Blunt yelled.

Hampton jumped up from the rocks. "Hold it, Blunt," he screamed.

Blunt fell in the saddle and spun his horse around, his eyes widening in instant fear. He grabbed for his pistol, jerking it from the holster.

Hampton fired, but the horse danced away and he missed.

Blunt squeezed off a shot, which pinged into the rock beside Hampton and sprayed him with chips of rock.

Blunt managed to rein his horse in, turn him toward safety and kick him savagely with his boot heels.

Hampton fired again. The bullet thudded home.

Blunt flung up his arms, losing his reins and throwing his pistol behind him.

Twice more Hampton squeezed the trigger and the bullets hit with sickening effect.

Blunt's ribs and chest dripped blood as he tumbled backward out of the saddle and crashed to the ground in a heap. His horse bolted over the rise, Hampton wasting a shot trying to bring it down.

Hampton bounded out of the rocks and ran to Blunt, kicking him with his boot. "Get up, you son of a bitch, so I can shoot you again," he screamed. In his rage, he thought he saw the body quiver, so he shoved the gun barrel in Blunt's open mouth and squeezed the trigger. The whole body jerked at the muffled explosion.

Hearing the sound of pounding hooves, he spun madly around and lifted his rifle.

"No," yelled Johnny Walls and Gibson simultaneously.

"Hugh," Gibson shouted, "we've got more trouble coming. Get in the rocks."

The sound of his name cut through the

rage and Hampton jumped for cover in the rock pile. From the house he heard screams and saw Blunt's two daughters jump for horses. Charlie grabbed her father's bewildered horse as it slowed in front of the house, while Josie untied one from the hitching rack. The women were mounted and charging toward the rock pile before Blunt's hired hands could react.

"What do we do, Hugh?" yelled Gibson as Davis ran to his side.

"If they shoot first," Hampton yelled, "kill them."

The women were halfway to the rocks before the Blunt men mounted and charged after them. "Fire at the men," Hampton yelled.

They released a volley, then another, but the men didn't slow. They charged on.

Charlie was almost at the rock pile when Josie's horse stumbled and threw her to the ground. Hampton looked from her to Charlie, who bounded down the incline, then reined up the horse at her father's body and jumped to the ground. She jerked the pistol at her side, and Hampton swung his carbine around to shoot her.

Screaming, Charlie fired her pistol once, twice, three times — all at the ground, all at her father's body, which twitched and jerked from the impact.

Hampton was shocked, even more so when she kicked and spat at her father. He was paralyzed in amazement until a bullet pinged off the rock nearby. Hampton twisted around to see the four Blunt hands closing the gap. He fired until his carbine was empty, then jerked his pistol.

He saw Josie struggling to get up from the ground, bullets kicking up dust all around her. She was going to get hurt.

Dropping his carbine, Hampton jumped from the cover of the rocks and darted toward Josie, zigzagging until he reached her. He stopped, fired his pistol at the nearest rider, shoved his arm under her shoulder and dragged her toward the rocks.

Gibson and Davis from the trees and Wall from horseback just behind the rock pile leveled a withering fire at the four men, driving them back toward the ranch house, providing cover for Hampton as he struggled to get Josie out of danger.

Hampton collapsed by the rock pile, but Josie fought to get free, then jumped up and pulled her gun. She screamed and Hampton thought she was about to point her pistol at him, but she lunged toward Charlie.

"Let me at him, dammit, let me at him," she cried, almost deliriously.

As Hampton watched, she emptied her pistol in him, then fell to her knees beside him and began to pummel his broken and battered body with her fists.

"You bastard," she screamed, "you damn bastard." She ripped at his clothes and rifled his pockets. Nothing seemed to assuage her rage.

Hampton was stunned. He looked from Josie and Charlie to Johnny Walls, who shook his head in disbelief. He gazed at Gibson and Davis, both frozen in shock. What about Blunt's allies? He spun around and dashed up the rise in time to see them scurrying for cover around the ranch house.

Transfixed by the savagery of Blunt's daughters, the men stood in motionless horror, listening to the two women sobbing with rage. When reality finally overcame the shock in Hampton, he shoved his pistol in his holster, then retreated to the rock pile and found his hat and carbine. He dusted off his hat before placing it on his head, then reloaded his carbine, glancing occasionally at the Blunt place to see what the hands might be planning. He saw them forting up in the barn and house, scurrying about for the attack they anticipated.

It was as he figured. Blunt's men had been cowards. They wouldn't fight an even fight.

They would cut and run once one of them was down. Hampton spat in disgust, then turned to Johnny Walls, motioning for him to fetch the two horses the Blunt women had ridden. Walls shrugged his failure to understand. "Their horses," Hampton called, "fetch their horses." Hampton pointed to the animals standing fifty yards away beneath a mesquite tree.

Nodding, Walls rode away, trailing the three horses still tied behind him.

From the trees where they had hidden and fought off the charge by Blunt's men, Gibson and Davis emerged hesitantly, staring wide-eyed at the women.

Charlie stood transfixed, glaring down at her father's body. On her knees, Josie had buried her face in her hands but still sobbed without control.

Hampton circled the women and met Walls as he trotted up with the two extra horses. Hampton took the reins and stepped softly toward the women. Charlie looked up from the ground, her dark eyes strangely tranquil. Hampton could not read her emotions, nor did he think she understood them herself. Despite all he had seen, despite the rumors that circulated about her and her sister, Hampton still found her comely. He lifted the reins and offered them to her.

Charlie's hand moved awkwardly toward his, gently pulling the reins from his fingers. She said nothing for a moment and though her eyes seemed to focus on his, she seemed to be staring at something distant, something beyond Hampton.

Words failed him. What could you say to a woman whose father you had just killed? Hampton thought. He turned away, stepping toward Walls.

"Thank you," she said softly.

Hampton turned around and nodded, uncertain whether she was thanking him for returning the horses or for killing her father.

"For the candy," she said.

Now Hampton stared blankly at her. He did not understand, after what she had just seen, how she would remember the horehound candy he had given her in Stanley's Mercantile. "Sure," he answered, then turned around and angled for Johnny Walls and the horses.

Gibson and Davis approached. Gibson patted Hampton on the shoulder, but said nothing. The three men untied their horses from the string, shoved their carbines in their scabbards, then mounted.

Hampton turned his chestnut about to look at Charlie. She seemed to be staring at him, but he could not be certain, not in the dim twilight. He turned his gelding, then touched his heel to the animal's flank. The chestnut trotted off toward his cabin . . . or what had been his cabin.

The men rode in a silent clump until the darkness was total and they could not see one another's faces. Hampton knew they were contemplating the savagery they had witnessed in the women. For the women to turn like that upon their father's body was proof, in Hampton's mind, that the rumors were true, that their father had indeed sold them to other men for carnal purposes. The two sisters had lived a life of fear for years, their pent-up rage finally exploding when they saw him dead and unable to carry out his threats.

When they reached the point where the trails split for their separate ranches, the men drew up their horses and shook hands all around. Nothing else needed to be said. Walls and Davis rode on, leaving Gibson and Hampton atop their horses.

Gibson spoke first "You don't have a place to go home to, do you?"

"Nope."

"You're welcome to stay with me and Matilda for a few days."

"Maybe tonight, but that's all," Hampton said.

The two men shook their reins and aimed the horses down the trail for Gibson's place.

"Damnedest thing I ever saw, those women. It bothers the hell out of me."

"They were like Comanche women over a dead enemy," Gibson replied. "Just one thing bothers me about the whole incident."

"What's that?"

"The Blunt women got a good enough look at each of us to turn us over to the law," Gibson replied.

14

Matilda Gibson rushed out the door in the darkness and threw her arms around her husband. "You're okay," she kept repeating, "you're okay. And the others?"

When Let Gibson spoke, his voice seemed to indicate he was embarrassed by his wife's display of affection in front of Hugh Hampton. "They killed Frank Winfrey last night," he said.

"My God," Matilda cried, "when will it end?"

"Lem Blunt's dead," Hampton answered.

"Then it's over," Matilda sighed.

"Maybe not," Hampton answered. "Blunt's daughters got close enough to identify us."

Matilda released her husband, then stepped to hug Hampton.

Let said, "I promised Hugh he could spend the night, since he's burned out of a place to live."

"He's welcome for as long as he likes."

Hampton shook his head. "I'll stay tonight. Tomorrow I start rebuilding."

Matilda slipped back to her husband and walked with him into the house. Hampton lingered outside, looking west where a bank of distant clouds glowed from lightning, then growled thunder that seemed farther and farther away, as if the cloud were dying. If the cloud loosed any rain, it would be too far away to do any good.

Hampton shook his head and stepped inside, where Matilda had lit a lamp before tossing and smoothing quilts on the floor for his bed.

"That'll do, Matilda. Come morning, I'll be leaving at first light."

"I'll fix breakfast," she offered.

He shook his head. "I've much work to do starting over. I want to get an early jump on it."

Matilda nodded and retreated from the parlor blowing out the lamp to give Hampton his privacy.

Hampton undressed slowly and fell upon the makeshift mattress, envying Gibson his wife. All his protestations to the contrary, Let was fond of Matilda and a better man because of her.

Despite his weariness, Hampton fought

sleep. The killing of Lem Blunt haunted him, not for his pulling the trigger, but for the savagery that he had witnessed by Blunt's daughters. He had always valued women for their civility, maybe because he had been around so few in his life. But those actions were no better than a man's, Hampton thought, recalling his own rage as he stood over Blunt's body. And yet, for all the savagery that drove Charlie and her sister to attack their father's body, Charlie had remembered to thank him for the candy. It was an odd paradox that Hampton couldn't resolve before he fell off to sleep.

Arising before dawn, he dressed quickly and left so Matilda would not take it upon herself to fix him breakfast, though his stomach growled for food. He rode his chestnut toward his ranch — or what was left of it. The sun was just topping the trees when he spotted the blackened remains of his cabin and barn. In the cabin he made out the bloated shape of his overturned, cast-iron cook stove, but nothing else. One blackened wall of the barn still stood, scorched and useless. After dismounting and tying his horse at a corner post of the corral, Hampton picked his way through the barn debris, kicking at the rubble. He uncovered the head of a shovel and toed at a scorched scrap of a canvas feed bag. There was nothing worth salvaging.

Shaking his head, he left the barn rubble and walked into the jagged skeleton of his demolished cabin. He toed at the heat-warped stove on its side, then kicked at the ashes and cursed his luck. He wondered whether to admit defeat and just ride on, leaving six years of hard work behind. If the drought didn't break, it mattered little what Hampton did. He could not survive.

Hampton grabbed his hat in anger and flung it toward the creek. He bent over, picked up blackened debris and threw it as far as he could, screaming until he was embarrassed by his foolishness. Then he strode quietly to the creek, picked up his hat and beat it against his britches.

Across the creek bed Hampton saw a blackened vee where the grass had caught fire after the bombing. The charred grass seemed to have consumed itself at the base of a mesquite tree not twenty yards away. Hampton had so wanted the fire to burn up Lem Blunt's grass, but even Hampton's bad luck seemed not to spread to the Lazy B.

At least Lem Blunt was dead.

Rather than mope about what might have been, Hampton decided to ride his place and herd as many cattle as he could to the few stagnant pools of water that remained along the creek. He marched back to the chestnut, untied it and mounted. The gelding trod wearily away from the burned shells of cabin and barn, its hooves kicking up plumes of dust beneath a sun that was turning fiery.

Hampton grimaced at what he saw. The cattle were scattered, resting in the shade of trees or nibbling individually on small clumps of grass. In places the ground, stripped of grass, was powdery from the repeated passing of hungry and thirsty cattle. Hampton counted more than thirty new carcasses, seven of them calves from the spring crop. Calves were the future of any rancher, and Hampton was beginning to wonder if he had a future.

A few yearlings and heifers looked strong enough to make it through the summer, but Hampton knew they would number no more than a hundred head by then and be so weakened as to take another year to breed. The drought would cost him two calf crops if it wasn't over soon.

Hampton looked to the sky, hoping he would find some sign of rain, some sign of hope.

There was none.

And if Charlie or Josie identified him as

their father's murderer, he stood less chance of making it through the summer than the yearlings and heifers.

Hampton had faith in Charlie. Despite the savagery he had witnessed, he believed her a decent woman tainted by an indecent father. Hampton had much less faith in Josie, though. People like Charlie had the fortitude to overcome a hard life. But some people adapted to mistreatment by harming others. Hampton worried that Josie had been ruined by her father and could never right her life. He hoped he was wrong for her sake — because she deserved a better shot at life — and for his own.

What cattle he could find, he began to drive toward the creek. They went reluctantly at first, bellowing and stamping their disapproval until they caught the scent of water and began to trot for the creek, kicking up dry, chalky dust.

Hampton shook the reins on the chestnut and guided him toward the shade of a pecan tree, flushing a jackrabbit from a clump of prickly pear. Hampton reached across his waist, jerked his pistol free and fired at lunch. The rabbit tumbled to the ground.

Hampton dismounted, tied his horse to the tree and retrieved the rabbit. Reaching into his britches, he pulled out his pocket-knife, then slit its stomach and pulled out its warm entrails. The jackrabbit was old and Hampton knew the meat would be tough, but it was still food. He tossed the rabbit onto a prickly pear pod and left it while he gathered wood and built a small fire. Finding a stick that would serve as a spit, he returned to the rabbit and finished skinning it, the meat making a crackling noise as it was separated from the hide. Hampton flung the hide aside, cut off the head and feet, then shoved the spit through the carcass.

Moving to the fire, he squatted and began to cook the purple meat. Gradually the meat browned as its juices dripped and splattered in the flame. When the meat was dark brown and crisp, Hampton pulled it from the flame and began to gnaw at it. As he expected, the meat was tough and lean. He ate what meat he could with his teeth, then used his knife to slice off bites that clung to the bone. As the carcass fell apart, he tossed the bones in the fire and leaned back against the pecan tree, letting the food settle. When he got up, he walked around the tree, picking up a dozen pecans that had lasted through the winter untouched by squirrels. He cut the hard shells with his knife and ate the meat inside. The pecans were dark and a mite bitter, but still helped to fill his stomach.

After the meager meal settled, he used his boot to mound dirt over the fire so there was no chance of setting the grass ablaze. He marched to his chestnut and took a drink of water from his canteen. The water tasted good, in spite of its warmth. He mounted up and headed off in the direction the cattle had taken.

After a short ride, he topped a hill and saw the cattle spread out before him in the creek bed. They were milling about in more mud than water, but that was the best he could provide. The cattle had hit the creek about two miles from his cabin site, and Hampton opted to follow the meandering creek bed back to his place. He told himself he would not let Lem Blunt or the drought defeat him, but he knew he must start rebuilding today, in spite of the searing heat, to prove it. As his demolished cabin came in sight around a final bend in the creek, he cursed a last time at the charred remains. A man could curse his fate forever or do something about it. Now was the time to start working and to quit cursing. Reaching the corral, Hampton dismounted and un-saddled his chestnut. Besides his weapons, saddle and saddlebags, all Hampton's possessions, other than what he wore, amounted to his bedroll and the war bag with a change of clothes and spare ammunition. Hampton threw the saddle over the top fence rail and fished into the saddlebag for his hobbles. He feared that Walls, in his excitement once the shoot-out started with Lem Blunt, might have forgotten to return the hobbles to the saddlebag. Hampton, though, found the hobbles easily. As he fished them out, his hand brushed against the Gillyards' Bible and the stick of dynamite dropped after the first attempt on his cabin. He wasn't sure what to do with the Bible, but he would dispose of the dynamite later if he didn't need it. He hobbled his horse so the gelding could graze on what grass remained along the creek bed, then moved to tear away the blackened remnants of the last two days.

He removed the bandolier from over his shoulder, then unbuttoned the bib on his shirt and pulled it over his head, exposing his muscled chest. He unbuckled his gun belt, then rebuckled it and hooked it over the fence post. With Lem Blunt dead, Hampton was not nearly as worried about being ambushed. Blunt's men had proved themselves to be nothing more than cowards after the old man's death. Hampton waded into the barn, looking for the remnants of tools he could use. He noted how the one wall still standing seemed to teeter. He jerked a partially burned rafter from the jumble of charred and scorched wood, then shoved against the wall, which withstood his assault. Hampton threw his weight into it three times before it gave a final groan and fell to the ground, kicking up a cloud of dust mixed with ash. Hampton coughed and swatted at the cloud enveloping him. He tossed the rafter down and stepped away from the rubble for a breath of fresh air.

Immediately, he heard the chestnut whinny. He looked around and grimaced. Sitting on horseback not twenty feet away were Sheriff Perry Johns with pistol drawn and County Attorney Royce Dugan with a shotgun aimed at Hampton's gut.

Shaking his head, Hampton lifted his arms. "I don't suppose you came out to learn who blew up my place? Or was it another cyclone and lightning strike?"

The sheriff shook his head and spat. "Came to arrest you for the murder of Lemuel Blunt."

"Don't know what you're talking about," Hampton shot back.

"We've got witnesses that say they saw you commit the murder," Dugan said.

Hampton's spirits sank. Dugan had said

"witnesses," and that meant Josie *and* Charlie must have spoken with the sheriff. Hampton wished for his pistol; then he could make a bid to escape. He knew he would die in the attempt, but it was a better, more honorable death than a death by hanging. Lem Blunt deserved to die at the end of a rope, not himself, thought Hampton. But then, the law in Brown County was so askew that right was wrong and wrong was right. Hampton knew he would have no justice under the law as it was practiced in Brown County.

Dugan dismounted, waving the shotgun at Hampton's belly. "You threatened Lem Blunt in my office," Dugan started, "and then caught up with him yesterday, killed him in cold blood. His hands saw it, and bless their hearts, his own two daughters saw it before you raped them. A despicable act for which I will see you convicted in a court of law and hanged in front of the courthouse."

"It's a lie," Hampton spat at the lawmen. "Frank Winfrey was murdered, too. You done anything about that?"

"You don't say?" Johns sneered at Hampton. "We'll just charge you with two murders, Hampton, and convict you of both."

Hampton started to say there were witnesses with him when he found Winfrey, but caught himself. He would not incriminate anyone else. "There was a shoot-out and Winfrey shot a Lazy B horse by the barn before he was killed."

Dugan laughed. "It ain't a Lazy B horse anymore. It was awfully ripe when we burned it this morning. Show him, Sheriff, so he'll believe."

Johns pulled a patch of horsehide from his vest pocket. Unfolding the stiff hide, Johns waved it at Hampton.

Hampton recognized a swatch of hair from a yellow dun. Then he saw the Lazy B brand.

"We cut it from the horse, just to make sure no one could identify it." Johns laughed.

Dugan lifted a pair of wrist shackles from over his saddle horn and advanced toward Hampton. "Look on the bright side of things, Hampton. With your cabin gone, we're offering you a place to stay and throwing in meals to boot, all of it free."

"And," the sheriff interjected, "we're gonna give you a necktie to wear at a big party. You'll be the center of attention and folks'll come from miles around to watch you take the first dance."

Dugan waved the shotgun at Hampton's

chest. "Give me your hands."

Hampton hesitated.

Dugan swung the shackles, the iron wrist bracelet striking Hampton against the side of the head, knocking his hat away.

Hampton staggered a moment and his eyes went blurry and watery as he tried to keep his balance.

Dugan growled. "The only thing keeping me from killing you now, Hampton, is that it'll raise fewer questions if I kill you legally in the courtroom." Dugan tucked the shotgun under his arm, then stepped close enough to grab Hampton's right wrist.

Shaking his head, Hampton felt the shackle snap around his wrist and knew he must do something, but his mind was still muddled. Before he could react and grab the shotgun, Hampton felt Dugan pull his other hand behind his back and lock it in the iron bracelet.

Hampton stood on wobbly knees, the bright sun blinding him. "What about my shirt and hat?" he managed.

"You won't be needing them," the sheriff said, dismounting. "Royce, you keep the shotgun on him while I fetch and saddle his horse."

"Glad to, Sheriff."

Hampton felt faint and let himself sink to

the ground so he wouldn't pass out. He lowered his head and shut his eyes, trying to block out the brightness, but it wasn't just the sun. Odd lights were still exploding in his head.

When he glanced up, he saw the sheriff saddling his horse, then inspecting his saddlebags for weapons.

"Well, I'll be damned, Royce," the sheriff called gleefully. "You won't believe what I just found."

Hampton tried to focus on what Johns held to the sky, but everything was a blur.

"Dynamite, a stick of dynamite." The sheriff laughed. "And, a Bible with the Gillyards' name in it."

"Damnation, Sheriff. It looks like Hugh Hampton wasn't just involved in the killings of Lem Blunt and Frank Winfrey, but in blowing the Gillyard brothers to hell as well, and maybe even killing Simon Levine."

Hampton cried out. "No, you bastards. I'll get a trial; I'll testify against everything you've said." He glanced up at Dugan, who lifted the shotgun in the air and slammed the butt at his head. Hampton dodged the blow, but it struck his shoulder and he screamed in pain as he collapsed on the ground.

"Who'd believe you, you son of a bitch?"

Dugan growled.

"I've got more evidence against Blunt and you two than you do against me," Hampton challenged.

"Perhaps," Dugan shot back, "but the difference is, we have plenty of time before trial to make up all the evidence we need."

Johns laughed. "That's why Royce Dugan is such a good county attorney."

Hampton watched Johns collect his carbine, gun belt and extra bandolier. The sheriff carried them to his own horse, where he tied them down. Then he approached Hampton, grabbing him under the shoulder Dugan had just smashed and jerking him to his feet.

Hampton gritted his teeth against the pain.

Johns shoved him roughly toward the chestnut gelding.

Hampton struggled to stay on his feet.

The sheriff shoved him again.

Hampton slammed into the corral fence, wincing at the agony. "Bastards," he said, his jaw clenched.

Johns laughed. "I would knock you out for using those kinds of words, Hampton, but then I'd have to tie you in your saddle and you might sleep through your parade in town." He shoved Hampton to the chestnut.

Hampton caught his breath as the sheriff grabbed his leg and shoved it in a stirrup, then boosted him into the saddle. For a dizzying moment, Hampton thought he was going to fall. His instincts told him to reach for the saddle horn to brace himself, but the shackles behind his back said no. He shut his eyes as the sheriff unhobbled the gelding. Finally, he felt the horse start to plod forward. When he opened his eyes, he saw a mounted Dugan leading his horse by the reins toward town.

It was a long, excruciating ride, his head awhirl with pain, his bare back roasting beneath the unforgiving sun. When he was finally led down the streets toward the jail, he heard people jeering. Two women picked up and threw handfuls of dirt at him. Why did they react so?

He passed one man who spat at him. "Rapist! You ought to be cut like a steer."

Hampton sighed. What kind of rumors had Johns and Dugan spread?

He had but a single hope: the lawyer Yantis.

15

The corner cell was one of four abutting the cold stone walls of the Brown County jail. The individual cells, each opened by a separate iron key, were squeezed in a narrow room behind the sheriff's office and separated from it by an iron door, locked and barred. The cells were dark, lit and ventilated only by the barred windows nine feet off the floor. Though the smallest cell, Hampton's was a corner cell with a side window onto the street as well as a back window.

Hampton lay upon his narrow bunk and thin mattress, which smelled faintly of urine. In the corner sat a bucket for relieving himself. The deputies smiled when they told him they emptied the bucket every other day.

Hampton's back burned from the shirtless ride into town, but his pride hurt even more with all the rumors the sheriff had spread about him. Gingerly, Hampton touched his head and shoulder, which still ached from the rough treatment by Dugan and Johns. He folded a woolen blanket to use as a pillow and stared at the dying shaft of light the setting sun cast on the wall.

Hampton had requested that the sheriff send for the lawyer Spencer Yantis, but Yantis had not come. Hampton wondered if Charlie and Josie had implicated Let Gibson, Johnny Walls and Spud Davis in their father's death. Their absence from jail gave him hope, though Hampton knew he may have been the first of the four arrested.

At a noise behind the iron door, Hampton sat up on his cot, propping his elbows on his knees and resting his head in his hands. Dizziness still bothered him. He heard the rattle of the key ring and the thud of an iron lock being opened. Hampton hoped the lawyer Yantis had arrived. When the door groaned open, he lifted his head, then dropped it back in his palms.

It was just a deputy carrying a tin plate. "Suppertime," he called as he approached. Squatting at the cell door, he dropped the plate on the floor and shoved it into the cell.

Hampton lifted his head long enough to see a cup of coffee, a bowl of thin soup, a hunk of fried ham, a potato and two slices of dry bread on the plate. The coffee and soup had sloshed out onto the bread and potato as well as a spot on the floor. There were no eating utensils.

"How about a knife and fork?"

The deputy stood up. "No knife, you might cut someone."

"What about a fork?"

"Sheriff says not. You might stab someone."

Hampton growled. "A spoon?"

"Sheriff's against it. Said you might dig your way out. How about using your fingers, unless you don't want any of it."

Hampton waved him away with a swipe of his arm.

"When you're done," the deputy taunted, "why don't you wash the tin in your slop pail?" The laughing deputy pointed at the waste bucket, then left. Too unsteady to walk the three strides to his supper, Hampton slid off the bed and crawled across the cold floor.

He picked up a slice of the coffee-soaked bread and shoved it in his mouth, hoping a little food in his stomach might help his aching head. Everything, including the coffee, was cold, but it was filling, which mattered more than taste. He picked up the tin of soup and gulped it down, its flavor so bland that he could not figure what kind of soup it could possibly be. He alternated bites of ham with potato until both were gone, then drank the coffee.

Hampton tried to stand up, but he slumped back to the floor. In frustration, he shoved the plate beneath the door and crawled back to his cot. He found the strength to push himself up, then collapsed onto the mattress, grimacing at the shoulder pain. He rolled over onto his left shoulder and stared at the wall as it gradually disappeared in the darkness. With night, the street noise picked up, as people emerged into the relative cool. From down the street Hampton could hear the sound of a saloon piano badly in need of tuning.

Though he was exhausted, rest eluded him. Perhaps he should have killed Charlie and Josie like he had killed their father, but those murders would have been neither lawful nor just. Blunt's death was not lawful, but it was just. His own death, if it came to a hanging, might be lawful, but it wouldn't be just.

The noise outside bothered him. He was used to living by himself, away from others and where the only noises were those of nature. Those noises were predictable, explainable. These sounds were as unpredictable as human nature. He turned over quickly, wincing at the pain in his shoulder, and trying to bury his head in the wool blanket he was using as a pillow. He thought he heard a hissing noise, followed by the soft call of his name. He lifted his head, wondering if he was imagining things until the noise came again.

"*Psssst, psssst!* Hampton. Can you hear me?" came the voice through the back window.

"Yeah," he called softly, so as not to raise the alarm of the sheriff and deputies. "Who is it?"

"Spencer Yantis," came the muffled reply.

"They're blaming me for things I didn't do."

"I know," Yantis answered. "You've still got friends. Someone's coming — I've got to run. I'll see you in the morning."

Then he was gone. Hampton felt encouraged, but that did nothing to ease the pain in his head and shoulder or drown out the street noise, which seemed to build louder and more menacing by the minute. Then it stopped suddenly, as if the world had come to a standstill. Hampton heard the sound of horses charging down the street and boots racing along the plank walks. A sinister silence prevailed for a moment, then came a low growl followed by the clamor of many voices.

Instantly, there was noise at the iron door as it was unbarred and unlocked. The deputy who had brought Hampton his supper jumped inside, carrying a sawed-off shotgun and two cartons of shells. "Okay," he shouted, and someone in the sheriff's office slammed the iron door shut, locked it, then passed the key through the barred peep window.

Despite the pain in his shoulder and head, Hampton sat up. "What's going on?"

The deputy spun around, his face barely visible in the light seeping in from the sheriff's office. "A lynch mob's coming. Menfolks are mighty upset about what you did to them Blunt girls after you killed their pappy."

"I didn't touch them," he shot back.

The deputy shrugged. "Tell that to a jury. I'm like the men outside. I want to see you hang, but my job's to protect you. Now do what I say." He pointed the shotgun at the barred windows in each cell. "They may try to get a ladder and somebody assassinate you through the window. If you hear a noise or spot anything there, you point it out to me. I'll pepper them with shot."

Hampton watched from window to window.

"If they get past the sheriff and county attorney at the front, I'll fight them off. I've the only key, so they can't get in."

"Send him out, send him out," the mob chanted.

The flames from their torches cast a flickering light through the high cell windows.

"Open up the jail and let us have him," a mob member yelled.

Through the barred peep window in the iron door, the deputy watched the front office. Hampton heard the growl of the mob and the men running and shouting around the jail. He heard whiskey bottles shattering against the stone wall outside.

"Send him out, send him out," the men shouted in unison.

A bottle broke across the iron bars of the window over his cot and splattered shards of glass across the floor. The deputy spun around, swinging his shotgun at the window but holding fire.

"You okay, Hampton?"

"Yeah."

"They won't get you unless they get me first." The deputy turned back around to the iron door. "The sheriff's opening up the front door. He and Royce Dugan are stepping outside to talk."

Hampton shook his head. He knew he was as good as dead with those two crooked bastards defending him from the mob.

The blast of a shotgun cut through the night and the noise, the crowd losing some of its exuberance but continuing to chant. "Send him out, send him out."

The chant was answered by another blast of the shotgun.

The chanting stopped.

Hampton heard the sheriff call out to the crowd. "Disperse and go home before some of you get hurt or killed. Nobody's taking this prisoner until he gets a fair trial."

"We heard what he did to the Blunt women," cried one. "He should die for that and for killing their father."

"I agree he should die," Perry Johns shouted, "but it's for a court to decide. I want to watch Hugh Hampton hang, but I want to do it in daylight when I can watch the expression on his miserable face. I want to do it in daylight surrounded by the respectable citizens that you can be, not the mob that you are now. I want him to die where women and children can watch and see what happens to the foul men who mistreat them."

Another mob member answered. "We want to see him die now."

He was answered by a voice Hampton recognized as Royce Dugan's. "You can wait until next week, can't you?"

Dugan was answered by silence.

"Well, can't you? Next week is when the district judge arrives. Hugh Hampton has several things to answer for, not just killing Lem Blunt and besmirching his daughters, but killing Simon Levine, Frank Winfrey and the Gillyard brothers."

Hampton screamed, "Liar. He's a damned liar."

"Shut up," the deputy yelled. "He's trying to save your hide."

"For a week, is all."

"It's more than you deserve."

The sheriff shouted to the crowd. "Now go back to your homes. You men, many of you have wives and children to think about. You want to be able to look them in the face in the morning and not have murder on your conscience."

"We're trying," yelled one of the mob, "to save our wives and daughters from him."

"As county attorney," Dugan yelled, "it'll be my job to prosecute any of you who participate in a lynching. The law will run its course, and as the prosecutor, I feel confident you will see in a week what you want done tonight."

"That's right," the sheriff added, "and let's not just hang him from a tree. Let's hang him from a scaffold we build on the courthouse square. Let him hear the sound of carpenters hammering it together. Every nail in the scaffold is a nail in his coffin."

The crowd murmured.

Sheriff Perry Johns addressed the crowd once more. "I'm breaking apart my shotgun and reloading. When I'm done, I'll count to ten. If you aren't dispersed by then, I'll do whatever it takes to send you home — even if your new home is with your Maker."

"One . . ."

The murmuring picked up and Hampton heard the snap of the shotgun as the sheriff opened it.

". . . two . . ."

"The bastard ain't worth us getting killed," yelled a nervous voice.

". . . three . . ."

"Time's running thin," Dugan shouted.

". . . four . . . five . . . six . . ."

Hampton heard the loud click of the sheriff snapping the shotgun together.

"Let's get out of here," came another voice.

Hampton heard a smattering of shouts

and men running down the street or along the plank walks. Another bottle was smashed against the stone side of the jail.

". . . seven . . . eight . . ."

Then a human stampede began, men running and shouting.

". . . nine . . ."

Hampton let out a long, slow breath. He would get his day in court to face the law, if not justice.

". . . ten!" the sheriff shouted.

The night exploded with one, then another shotgun blast.

"He scared them away," the deputy laughed as he turned around to Hampton. "You owe your life to the sheriff, a good lawman."

Hampton could only shake his head as he heard Dugan and Johns reenter the office and slam the door. The two men laughed.

"Did you see them turn tail and run, Royce?" asked the sheriff.

"Yeah, especially the one who fell into the water trough."

Hampton saw the sheriff at the window in the iron door. "Hand me the key, Deputy, and I'll let you out."

The deputy fumbled for the key and finally poked it through the window. The sheriff twisted the key in the lock and swung the door open.

As the deputy strode through the door, Johns patted him on the shoulder. "Any problems?"

"Nothing, except a bottle came through the window and shattered over the prisoner's floor."

"We'll give him the broom and let him sweep it up tomorrow," Johns said. "You take your shotgun and go stand out front, let me know if anything develops."

"Yes, sir," the deputy said.

As the deputy left, Hampton watched the sheriff enter the cell room. Johns clung to the darkness, fumbling with something that Hampton could not figure out until he saw a match flame. The sheriff lifted the match to his lips and for a moment Hampton could see his beady eyes in the ball of light. When the tip of his cigarette burned orange, Johns flipped the match toward Hampton. The match made an arc through the bars of Hampton's cell, then died before it hit the floor.

"Aren't you gonna thank me and the county attorney?" Johns sneered. "We saved your life tonight."

"You're spreading lies about me and you know it."

Johns laughed. "We'll let a judge and jury

decide that. I'll abide by whatever they determine."

"I know what you and Dugan have been doing, and I know you looked the other way for Blunt's mischief," Hampton shouted as he wadded his fingers into fists.

"Who'd believe you, especially after I risked my life tonight to save you from the mob? Hell, the county attorney was at my side, standing up for the rule of law against the rule of the mob."

Hampton fell back on the cot.

"You're a disgrace to the laws of Texas, Sheriff; did you ever think about that?"

"Can't say that I have, Hampton. Have you ever thought what it's like to be dead?"

Hampton didn't answer because he had no answer.

"Let me tell you, Hugh Hampton," the sheriff said, his voice low and menacing, "you're dead. You may still be breathing, but you're as good as dead." He spun around and strode out of the room, slamming the door behind him.

16

Day broke quiet and still. The jail, with its thick stone walls and high ceiling, was surprisingly cool. Hampton's shoulder was tender and his head was sore to the touch.

Hampton feigned sleep when the deputy came in at good light carrying a tin cup. He ran the cup against the steel bars, making a terrible clatter that bounced off the stone walls.

The deputy shoved a broom through the bars and it tumbled against Hampton's cot. "Time to get up, Hampton, and greet the sunrise . . . one of the few you've got left."

Hampton stretched in his bed, then turned over and stood up, glass crunching beneath his boots. He was glad now that he had been too tired and sore last night to pull them off.

"Sweep up the glass, then I'll bring your breakfast."

Hampton grabbed the broom and began

to sweep the thick plank floor.

"When you're done with that and done tending your morning business, get the slop bucket and leave it by the door. The cook needs it for lunch," the deputy taunted.

"It'd have more flavor than supper last night."

The deputy growled and exited, leaving the iron door open. Hampton pushed the shattered glass to the cell door and retreated to the corner.

The sheriff poked his head in the door as Hampton finished with the slop bucket and carried it to the cell door.

"The county attorney's convened the grand jury for today. A lot of the same men who were in the mob last night are on the grand jury." He shook his head. "It don't look good for you. They'll indict you for murdering Lemuel Blunt. We've got eyewitnesses on that. They could indict you for raping the Blunt girls, though Dugan may save that one. And, they'll likely indict you for murdering Simon Levine, too."

Hampton shook his head. "I didn't touch Blunt's daughters and you know Blunt killed Levine and sold his matched grays to the livery stable. I saw Blunt with Levine's money pouch, in fact."

The sheriff laughed. "You mean this

money pouch?" He pulled a leather pouch from behind his back, holding it so Hampton could see the Star of David on the side.

Hampton felt his shoulders slump.

"Besides the dynamite and the Gillyards' Bible, I found this in your saddlebags. You know whose it is?" The sheriff licked his lips.

"Levine's," he said in defeat.

"And by the way, the liveryman told me that you're the one that sold him the grays." The sheriff laughed. "See if Lawyer Yantis can get you out of this one, Hugh. I let him know this morning you were in a bit of a bind." The sheriff slammed the door.

Hampton retreated to the cot and lay down. He had never felt more alone in all his life.

The deputy returned in a half hour with breakfast. "Stay on your cot until I say otherwise," he ordered as he unlocked the cell door and kicked it open.

Hampton considered attempting to overpower the guard, but with his tender shoulder he knew he didn't have the strength to succeed. First he would talk to the lawyer Yantis, and if the situation was as bleak as it appeared, he would bide his time, then try to escape.

The guard took the broom and finished

sweeping the glass into the walkway, then lifted the slop bucket and locked the cell door behind him. "You can eat now."

Hampton fetched the plate and looked at a cold fried egg, two pieces of bacon and two slices of bread with mold around the edge. "No eating utensils?"

"Sheriff's orders," the deputy replied as he left.

Hampton started eating with his fingers and was finished by the time the deputy returned with the slop bucket.

"Keep your seat," the deputy ordered as he unlocked the door, slid the slop bucket inside, then locked up the cell again. "See you around lunchtime."

Hampton reclined on the cot, staring at the ceiling for a long time. He estimated it was almost noon when the iron door opened and Spencer Yantis walked in. The lawyer was stripped to his shirt, pants and socks, apparently to prevent him from slipping a weapon in beneath his clothes. He carried a sheaf of papers and a pencil.

"How about a stool?" Yantis asked the deputy.

Hampton arose to thank the lawyer for coming. "I'm obliged."

Yantis shook his head. "Don't thank me yet. At least wait until I remove your neck from the hangman's noose. Pull your cot over by the bars," he instructed as the deputy brought him a stool.

Hampton tugged the bed to the bars and sat down on the end opposite where Yantis placed his stool.

"Now, in case nobody's told you, Hugh, you were indicted for two murders this morning by the grand jury."

Hampton shook his head and started to speak.

Yantis held up his hand. "Don't say a thing just yet, and when you do, whisper. I don't want the sheriff overhearing anything we say. The indictments are for the murders of Lem Blunt and Simon Levine." Yantis lowered his voice to a whisper. "I know you didn't kill Levine, but did you shoot Blunt?"

Hampton licked his lips, but said nothing.

"I'm the only hope you've got, Hugh. You better level with me if you want to get out alive."

Pursing his lips, Hampton nodded.

"Good for you," Yantis whispered. "He'd needed killing for years. He's abused and controlled the laws to his benefit. Losing his claim to the land along Pecan Creek was the first time he hadn't been able to intimidate or buy the law."

"Let me ask you something," Hampton

whispered. "Was anybody else indicted in those murders?"

"No, sir."

Hampton sighed in relief.

"I take that to mean others were involved," Yantis remarked.

Hampton nodded.

"Care to tell me who?"

"Not really," Hampton replied, "or not just yet, at least."

Yantis stroked his chin. "If I tell you I need to know, I trust you'll tell me."

Hampton ignored the statement. "What are my chances of getting out of this?"

Yantis leaned back and clasped his fingers behind his neck. "Not good, Hugh, not good. A lot of townfolks want your blood. The mob last night should've shown you that." Yantis laughed, then looked over his shoulder. "Blunt's men riled up the crowd, telling things you're supposed to have done with Blunt's daughters. Johns was behind it all. He didn't care to see you lynched; his purpose was to stir feelings high enough so that men chosen to the jury will already have their minds made up."

"Bastard."

"Ain't he though," responded Yantis. "Now, the witnesses before the grand jury were Blunt's men — a Bibb Aultrong, Olean

Evans, Cyrus McCurdy and Ivey Yates — plus the old man's daughters, Josie and Charlie."

Hampton bit his lip at Charlie's name, disappointed that she had testified against him.

"Now," Yantis whispered, "this is important. Did any of them actually see you shoot Lem Blunt?"

"No, sir."

"Did any of them get close enough to see you?"

"The two women. I killed Blunt behind a slope that screened me from the house, and they came charging to see what had happened. We couldn't bring ourselves to shoot women. Odd thing is, they rode past us and began to attack their dead father. Never saw anything stranger than that in all my life."

"If you were hidden, did any of the four men see you?"

Hampton nodded. "Josie was thrown from her horse, stunned a moment. I feared she would get hit, and ran to pull her to cover. They could've recognized me then, but we drove them back before they could get close enough to identify anyone else."

Yantis made some notes on his paper. "The sheriff's already convinced folks you ravished Blunt's daughters. That's what's riled up the town the most."

"It's a lie."

Yantis shrugged. "So's most of the evidence against you, but we've got to disprove it and that may be hard to do."

"It's a lie, Spencer. You've got to believe me on this."

"Oh, I believe you, though a lot of folks don't. These are the same folks who looked the other way when Blunt murdered his wife and when word began to come out that he was bedding his daughters and offering them to any man who would take them."

Hampton grabbed the iron bars. "If I don't stand a chance, I want to know now so I can try to escape. I'd rather be shot in the back than hung by the neck."

Yantis shook his head. "You've got a chance — maybe one in a hundred or maybe one in a thousand. It's not good unless we can get some outside help. The district judge is Gregory Williams. He's a decent man, honest judge. We've six days before he arrives. Your trial will come up first."

It seemed hopeless to Hampton. His only chance was an escape, the sooner the better.

Scratching his chin with one hand, Yantis scribbled a note with the other on the paper.

"Tell me this, Hugh. Over the last week we've had two bombings and the murders of five men — Blunt, Winfrey, Levine and the two Gillyards."

Hampton nodded.

"Sounds like a state of anarchy beyond the control of our lawmen," Yantis said. "I intend to telegraph the governor to see if he can send in the Texas Rangers."

"What good can they do?"

"It'll keep the sheriff and county attorney looking over their shoulders." Yantis arose and folded his notes. "Don't lose your spirit."

"It isn't easy," Hampton replied.

"I know. I'll be back as I need you," Yantis said, standing and turning for the iron door. He stopped and retreated back to Hampton. "One other thing," he whispered. "Don't try an escape — unless I tell you to."

17

Hearing the voice of Spencer Yantis in the sheriff's office, Hugh Hampton pulled his cot toward the cell's iron bars. He had grown accustomed to these morning meetings, though he had begun to doubt their value. For the first time in the five days since their initial jail meeting, the lawyer wore a smile — if not his coat, tie and shoes, which the sheriff insisted he remove outside.

Yantis carried a stool in one hand and a stack of papers in the other. As he set the stool down opposite Hampton, he nodded. "Judge Williams arrived in town last night. I had a good conversation with him." Yantis extracted a folded piece of paper from his shirt pocket. "Just got a telegram. My request for Texas Rangers has been approved. We'll only get two, but at least that will be two honest lawmen, two more than we have right now in Brown County."

Hampton lashed out at Yantis. "What good

are they against a stacked deck and the rigged hand I've been dealt?" He bounced up from his cot and stalked about the cell like a caged animal. He thumped his whisker-stubbled cheek. "I'm not even allowed a bath or a shave." He slapped at his trousers then grabbed at his shirt. "I haven't been allowed a change of clothes since I've been here. Is this how I am going to be dragged into court tomorrow, looking like a saddle tramp?" He kicked the end of his cot. "Is this justice?"

"This," responded Spencer Yantis, "is Brown County."

Hampton lunged across the cell, clenching his fists around the iron bars. He whispered low to Yantis, "You told me not to attempt an escape until you said so. I'm running out of time. The trial's tomorrow. How long will it take? A day?"

"Likely two," Yantis answered calmly.

Hampton spun about and strode to the corner of the cell. "I haven't seen anyone except you, and I don't know if I've got another ally out there."

Before Yantis could respond, Hampton heard the noise of the iron door to the cell room being unlocked. The door groaned as it was pushed open by the sheriff. Johns entered, followed by Royce Dugan and a slender man Hampton had never seen before. Dressed in a suit, the man wore reading glasses on a chain around his neck. The widow's peak in his gray hair gave him a high forehead and a distinguished look.

Yantis stood up from his stool. "Good morning, Judge Williams. Thank you for coming by."

The judge nodded.

Hampton looked to Yantis for an explanation, but received none as the lawyer walked to the judge.

"Mr. Yantis," said the judge, staring down his long nose, "do you always go about barefoot and with your shirt hanging out?"

"That's the only way the sheriff lets me see my client, Your Honor."

The judge turned slowly to Perry Johns.

"Further," Yantis continued, "the honorable sheriff does not allow my client to have any eating utensils with his meals — not even a spoon, mind you."

"He's dangerous," Johns responded, "and might use them as weapons."

"Even a spoon?" the judge asked.

The sheriff did not respond.

Yantis pointed to the corner. "Hugh, fetch your slop bucket."

Hampton retreated to the rank bucket of waste, then carried it to his cell door and held it up against the iron bars.

"The sheriff," said Yantis, "does not empty this but once every two or three days."

"Is that true?" Williams asked Johns.

"My deputy must've forgotten."

"And," added Yantis, "despite repeated requests by me and by my client that he be allowed to shave, bathe and receive a change of clothes, the sheriff has denied him that simple decency."

The judge pursed his lips and nodded. "You've made your point, Mr. Yantis." He turned to the sheriff. "These requests are not unreasonable. See that they are met — a spoon for his meals and an opportunity for him to clean up."

Johns nodded.

The judge spun around and departed the cell area, Dugan walking out after him. "We'll attend these matters, Your Honor," called the county attorney after him.

The sheriff glared at Yantis, then spit toward the slop bucket as Hampton lowered it. "Bastard," he scowled, then left the room.

Yantis grinned at Hampton, then sat back down on the stool.

Hampton shook his head and started to apologize.

"Don't worry about it. Your life is at stake."

Hampton pushed his cot back to where it had been before he kicked it, then sat facing Yantis.

The lawyer leaned toward the cell. "You've friends outside, Hugh. Folks that know you, know you did not ravish Blunt's daughters. They'll be in the courtroom, but I've discouraged anyone from trying to see you. The less the sheriff and Dugan know about who're your friends, the better chance we'll have if you have to make an escape."

Hampton nodded.

"Now," Yantis said, "I am going to make a few statements. If the statements are wrong, tell me. If they are right, do not say a thing. I've got to handle it this way." Yantis leaned forward.

"Go ahead," Hampton whispered.

"You weren't alone when you killed Lem Blunt."

Hampton said nothing.

"The men with you were the same ones that came to my office after the Gillyard killings — excepting Frank Winfrey, of course."

Hampton sat silently.

"No one else was with you."

Hampton did not move a muscle.

Yantis nodded. "That tells me all I need to know."

"What are my chances, Spencer?"

The lawyer stood up and paced before Hampton's cell. "I'd be lying if I said good. It just depends on who the jury believes. The case against you is built on lies. They know it and you and I know it. If none of them actually saw you kill Lemuel Blunt, then I can prove inaccuracies in their accounts. The problem is, if they believe the rumors about what you did to Charlie and Josie, then the facts of the killing won't matter. The Blunt women are supposed to come into town tonight so they can testify. I figure Dugan will save them for last, since they'd make the most powerful witnesses."

Hampton let out a slow breath.

"Judge Williams is an honest and decent man, as you saw. The Texas Rangers are supposed to arrive tonight. Because of the high feelings about your case, I've asked the judge that the Rangers be assigned to stand guard in the courtroom throughout the trial. He has agreed. All weapons will be checked at the door.

"I plan to go back to the judge this afternoon and request that you be accompanied to and from the courthouse by a Ranger. That was one reason I wanted him to see your condition this morning, to build my case for why that is necessary. My biggest worry is that if I get you an innocent verdict, Perry Johns or Royce Dugan might find a way to do you harm."

Hampton shook his head. "I can fend for my own, except against the hangman."

Yantis reached through the cell bars and shook Hampton's hand. "If the judge goes along with my request for a Ranger to escort you, I'll see you in the courtroom in the morning. If the judge refuses, I'll be here to walk across the street with you and the sheriff."

"If I get out of this bind, Spencer . . ."

The lawyer held up his finger. "*When* you get out of this," he corrected.

"When I get out of this bind, I may have to give you my land, but I'll repay you."

"If we can bring down Sheriff Johns and the county attorney, I'll be repaid in full."

Yantis started for the iron door, then paused. "The sheriff should bring you a tub of water to bathe and shave in this afternoon. I've taken the liberty of asking Claude Stanley down at the mercantile to provide you a new suit of clothes, shirt, tie, socks, everything. He's agreed. Everything'll work out . . . I hope."

Nodding, Hampton shoved his cot back in place and threw himself upon it. The closer it came to reaching trial, the longer it seemed for time to pass. He had come to hate the waiting as much as the prospect of hanging.

Noon came and went without so much as a crumb for a meal. In the middle of the afternoon, the iron door opened up and the deputy and sheriff toted in a tub of water. They set it in the vacant cell beside him, then placed a bar of soap and a straight razor on the floor beside it.

"What about a towel?" Hampton asked.

"Air'll dry you off," the sheriff answered.

The deputy retreated, then brought in a pile of new clothes he set by the cell door.

"What about lunch?" Hampton called to the sheriff as he started to leave.

"Glad you asked, you son of a bitch." He shoved his hand in his pants pocket and jerked out a spoon. "The judge said I should give you a spoon for your meals, but he didn't say anything about food." Johns tossed the spoon into Hampton's cell, then left laughing.

The deputy placed the new clothes on the stool Yantis used for his conferences. "Take off your clothes," he commanded.

Hampton began to strip.

"I'll open this cell and you move to the next and I'll lock you in while you clean up."

When he was naked, the deputy motioned for him to back away from the door. As Hampton obeyed, the deputy unlatched the lock. Hampton walked from his cell to the next, closing the door behind him. As the deputy locked the cell, Hampton lowered his buttocks into the tub, which was big enough for him to sit in but not for him to put his legs in. His feet rested on the floor.

The water was cool and he lathered up and washed away layers of dirt, grime and smoke, feeling better by the moment. He lathered his face well, then took the razor and scraped off his whiskers as best he could without a mirror.

As he cleaned up, the deputy removed the slop bucket, then began a search of Hampton's cell.

"What do you expect to find?" Hampton asked.

"Anything the lawyer might have passed you."

Hampton laughed. "You won't find anything."

In ten minutes, the deputy emerged from the cell, disheartened that Hampton had been right. "Hurry up," the deputy ordered.

Hampton leaned forward in the tub. "You want to come in and wash my back?"

The deputy scowled.

After rinsing his hair and head a final time, Hampton washed his legs and stood up, the air cool upon his wet flesh.

There being no towel, Hampton stepped to the cot in the cell and picked up a folded blanket, shook it loose and began to dry himself.

"Dammit," the deputy cried.

"Should've given me a towel." He took extra time to dry.

"Slide the razor out," the deputy commanded, "then I'll open your cell and let you return to your cot."

Hampton obliged. "What about a comb?"

"Not after you messed up the blanket."

Hampton shrugged and ran his fingers through his hair, trying to straighten it.

The deputy unlocked the door, then backed away, motioning for Hampton to return to his cell.

Hampton walked in, stooping to pick up the new clothes.

The deputy slammed his cell door and quickly locked it. The deputy dragged the tub of soapy water out of the room and shut the iron door.

Hampton began to dress, putting on clean long johns, but deciding not to wear the shirt and suit until the morning. He did straighten his clothes out on his cot, his hand feeling a piece of paper as he brushed a wrinkle out of the suit coat. He slid his hand in the pocket and pulled out a white sheet of paper, folded in half.

Opening the paper, he saw a note. It read, "We're with you, Hugh." It was signed by Claude Stanley.

Hampton sat on the floor and leaned back against the cool stone wall. Now all he could do was wait and hope the lawyer Yantis could pull off a legal miracle.

By late afternoon, his stomach was cramping from hunger. He knew the sheriff was toying with him, so he did not complain.

The only interruption the rest of the afternoon was when he heard a noise at the barred window in the iron door. He saw Dugan staring at him.

"Here's your father's killer, on the floor, sitting against the wall," he said.

Hampton saw the face of Charlie Blunt briefly through the opening. Hampton cursed at himself, wondering why he hadn't killed her when he had the chance.

After she left, Hampton hoped for supper as he toyed with the spoon, even though he knew he would be denied meals after Yantis had humiliated the sheriff in front of the judge.

Well after dark, he tried to go to sleep, but

the hunger and the anxiety gnawed at him until he was startled by the sound of gravel being tossed at the barred window over his cot.

"What?" he called softly.

He heard something hit one of the window bars and then fall to the floor beside his cot. He rolled to the floor and fumbled around until he found a paper package tied in twine.

Quickly, he unwrapped it and felt inside. It was too light to be a weapon, but what was it? Food! Squares of some kind of food. He lifted the package to his nose and caught the aroma of horehound candy.

18

Hugh Hampton was dressed and waiting when the iron door opened. Sheriff Perry Johns, a pair of shackles in his hand, marched in ahead of a lean lawman with a wide mustache and narrow eyes. By the badge on his chest, Hampton recognized him as a Texas Ranger. Hampton grinned. The judge had agreed to Yantis's request.

Again this morning the sheriff had not provided him a meal, but the horehound candy that had been thrown through the window had satisfied the hunger pangs, if not his appetite.

The sheriff unlocked the cell and motioned for Hampton to step forward. Hampton lifted his hands and obliged, the sheriff quickly clamping the shackles upon his wrists.

"You ready to go to hell, I mean to trial?" Johns taunted.

"When I inform the judge you haven't

given me a meal since he visited me yesterday morning, we'll see who's in trouble."

Johns jerked Hampton out of the cell and shoved him toward the iron door. Johns reached to shove him again, but the Texas Ranger grabbed his fist.

"He's my prisoner now," the Ranger said in a low, menacing voice, "so back off, Sheriff."

Johns withered under the Ranger's hard glare.

The Ranger, his Winchester in his right hand, clasped his left hand firmly upon Hampton's arm and guided him through the iron door and the sheriff's office out onto the walk. Outside, the Ranger released Hampton's arm and lifted the Winchester, holding it across his chest so no one would doubt his serious intent.

Activity on the street stopped. Men and women, many of them standing in the shade of the trees on the courthouse square, looked and pointed. From down the street ran others to get a look at Hampton and the Ranger. Hampton could feel their cold, hateful stares as some men took menacing steps to cut off the path to the courthouse.

"Clear the way," yelled the Ranger as he stepped off the plank walk. He glanced back over his shoulder at Hampton. "Stay at my side. If you see anyone go for a gun, you drop to the ground. I'll take care of him."

Hampton nodded and followed the lawman across the street toward the courthouse. Though several men made threatening gestures and jeered at Hampton, none challenged the Ranger, who reached the courthouse and opened the door for his prisoner to enter. The Ranger pointed him up the stairway, where several men loitered.

"Move along," the Ranger ordered, "so we can pass."

One man hesitated.

"Now," the Ranger growled.

The man dashed up the stairs and Hampton followed. At the head of the stairs, the hallway was crowded as men and women made their way to the courtroom. Hampton passed the county attorney's door, remembering with disgust his meeting there with Dugan, the sheriff and Blunt.

"Out of the way," the Ranger said.

"Look," called a woman, "here he comes."

Turning to stare, people backed against the wall as the Ranger held out his rifle to clear a path. With his rifle, the Ranger pushed a couple men out of the doorway. They started to protest, then wilted beneath his gaze. The Ranger allowed Hampton to slide on into the courtroom, where another

Texas Ranger stood at a table by the door, collecting weapons and searching people.

The courtroom held a hundred people comfortably, and there were half again that many already crowded inside. The room sweltered with the humid heat of so many bodies. The room was awhirl with motion, women waving fans, men shaking their hats. The lucky ones sat by the tall windows, opened to their full height, and savored what little breeze there was.

Behind the empty jury box, one window was shaded by the branch of a tall pecan tree that came within two feet of the court-house. Hampton studied it as he walked down the aisle. If he was convicted, he would attempt to escape out the window and down the tree. He would much rather die from a gunshot to the back than a noose around his neck. He shivered at the thought of strangling to death.

Among the crowd he saw Let and Matilda Gibson, who was sweating profusely, near the front. To one side he saw Johnny Walls and his newlywed bride. On the other side of the room he saw Spud Davis. He wondered why none of them were seated together.

On the other side of the knee-high railing he saw Spencer Yantis leaning over his table.

When Yantis straightened, he smiled and strode to meet Hampton, shaking his shackled hand and slapping him on the shoulder. As Yantis bent to open the gate at the end of the aisle, Hampton saw out of the corner of his eye a woman arise from the front row near the jury box.

Instantly, the crowd hushed.

Hampton looked around, then back at the woman. She was tall and bronzed with her black hair done in a bun. Her shapely body fit nicely in the blue chambray dress with a button-up collar. At first Hampton did not recognize her, because he had never before seen Charlie Blunt in a dress.

She stared straight at him.

He looked into her dark, inscrutable eyes and could read them no more than he could read Latin. He clenched his jaw, wondering why he hadn't killed her with her father, yet at the same time glad he hadn't.

Betraying no emotion, she lifted her right hand to her mouth, pausing for a moment, then slid something between her lips. Then she slowly sat down, her gaze never leaving his. What was her motive? Was she taunting him? Was she trying to tell him something? Or, was he imagining things?

He stared at her as he walked past Yantis to the defendant's table. The crowd murmured about the silent exchange between them.

Yantis was quick behind him. "What was that all about?" he whispered.

Hampton shook his head. "I don't know."

"I wish I knew how she planned to testify," the lawyer said, pulling back the chair for Hampton. "She's a calculating woman, much shrewder than her younger sister. I figure Dugan will save her for his last witness. He'll start with Blunt's men."

The lawyer leaned closer to Hampton. "My strategy is to prolong the trial so Charlie Blunt won't testify until tomorrow morning. That'll give me time to figure out any ploys Dugan may have and how to counter her accusations. And, if things look bad, we'll know to plan your escape."

Hampton jerked his head toward Yantis. "You wouldn't go outside the law when we first approached you. Why now?"

Nodding, Yantis studied Hampton. "You're an innocent man."

A door behind the judge's bench opened and Judge Gregory Williams came out wearing a black suit and tie over a white shirt. He closed the door behind him and stepped to the bench. Before he sat down, he stared at the crowd and pulled a revolver from the holster beneath his coat.

"Because of the extraordinary lawlessness in Brown County the last month, this trial will be conducted on very strict terms — my terms." He held the revolver in front of his chest long enough for all to see, then placed it on the bench. "There will be no outbursts, no chattering, no disruptions of any type from the spectators, or the court will be cleared. All weapons are to be left at the back of the room under the supervision of the Texas Rangers. Any man or woman who brought a weapon, gun or knife, into this room without checking it at the door is subject to a jail sentence. If you've a weapon hidden on you, you best check it now."

Two men stood up and retreated to the Ranger at the door.

"To help maintain order, we have the assistance of two Texas Rangers, Jason Michael at the back and Scott Lewis at the front."

Lewis, the Ranger who had escorted Hampton from the jail, marched past Hampton's table and stood by the judge's bench.

"Any, and I mean *any* disruption, intentional or unintentional, will be dealt with severely," the judge continued

Williams took his seat and turned to Royce Dugan. "Is the state ready in the case of the People versus Hugh Hampton on two counts of murder?"

"The state is prepared, Your Honor."

Williams turned to Yantis. "And, is the defense prepared?"

"Yes, Your Honor."

Williams nodded at Hugh Hampton. "Will the defendant please rise."

The sound of Hampton's chair sliding on the hardwood floor was the only sound in the hushed courtroom as he stood.

"How do you plead on the count of murder in the death of Simon Levine?"

"Not guilty," he said adamantly.

"How do you plead on the count of murder in the death of Lemuel Blunt?"

"The same, not guilty."

"Thank you, be seated. If there are no motion on the two counts, we will move to select a jury."

Spencer Yantis rose from his chair. "Your Honor," he said, "defense moves to dismiss the first count of murder in the death of Simon Levine."

"Upon what grounds, Mr. Yantis?"

Yantis strode toward the bench, then turned to face Royce Dugan.

"Your Honor, the state has failed to produce the corpse of Mr. Levine. Mr. Levine is an itinerant peddler who is known to travel all over the state of Texas. For all we know, he may well be in Comanche County or Taylor County. If Mr. Levine is dead, as the state claims, then Mr. Dugan must know where the body is." Yantis pointed his finger like a pistol at Dugan. "How did Mr. Levine meet his death, Mr. Dugan?" Yantis shrugged. "Where is the body, the corpse, the skeleton, the remains, Mr. Dugan, where?"

Yantis smiled and returned to his seat, Dugan's hateful eyes watching him the entire way. As Yantis sat down, Royce Dugan rose, his face haughty, his bearing condescending.

"The bench awaits your response, Mr. Dugan," said the judge. "Where is your evidence?"

Except for the rattle of the shackles as Hampton twisted in his chair to watch Dugan, the room was silent.

Dugan moved cautiously around his table, staring to the front row of spectators where the Lazy B hands sat. Hampton saw Bibb Aultrong cautiously lift his hand like a bashful schoolboy, then glanced at Dugan, whose face flushed instantly and whose eyes widened. "No," he shouted instantly, and Aultrong's hand slid down in his lap. "No," Dugan repeated and turned around to the judge, "the state does not have the body of Simon Levine, that is correct, but what we have is a pattern of unlawful conduct on the part of Hugh Hampton that builds to the logical conclusion he was involved in the murder of Simon Levine, if not several other Brown County residents over the past month."

As he spoke, Dugan seemed to grow invigorated at the challenge of countering Yantis's assertions. "Though the state does not have the body of Simon Levine, it does have his distinctive money pouch, found in the saddlebags of Hugh Hampton when the sheriff and I arrested him for the murder of Lemuel Blunt."

Yantis slowly arose from his seat. "Your Honor, I can produce a witness who will state under oath that that pouch was first seen in the possession of Lemuel Blunt, and only after his death did it appear in Mr. Hampton's saddlebags."

Dugan stepped toward the bench. "Your Honor, I can produce a witness who says Mr. Hampton sold the matched grays of the presumed-dead Mr. Levine at the livery stable."

Yantis shook his head. "Your Honor, I can produce a witness who will state under oath that Lemuel Blunt sold those horses to the livery stable, not Mr. Hampton."

Dugan stalked around the table and looked at his notes.

Yantis sat down and smiled at Hampton.

Hampton shook his head and leaned over to his lawyer. "Where'd you find these witnesses?" he whispered.

Yantis leaned over and whispered, "I didn't. I made them up." Very solemnly, the lawyer straightened in his chair.

Hampton grinned, his confidence growing, particularly as he glanced at Aultrong, who didn't think as logically as most men. Yantis could easily trip up Aultrong on the witness stand.

"Mr. Dugan," Judge Williams began, "do you care to show any reasons why I should not dismiss the count of murder in the presumed death of Simon Levine?"

Dugan sighed as he turned around and strode to the bench. "Your Honor," he bellowed, "the state admits it has but a thread of evidence in Mr. Levine's death."

"Presumed death," the judge corrected.

Chastised, Dugan nodded. "Presumed death. But the state believes it is one thread in the fabric of mayhem and terror Hugh Hampton has tried to throw around this county."

Yantis stood up and spoke very softly.

"Your Honor, please accept the defendant's humble request for dismissal of the charge for a death of which we have no body."

Williams picked up his gavel and slammed it against the bench. "The charge is dismissed."

Yantis sat back down in his chair and leaned over to Hampton. "Getting you off the next charge," he said, "won't be nearly as easy."

19

The rest of the morning was spent in jury selection. Hampton, his confidence growing in Spencer Yantis, paid less attention to the process than to the window behind the jury box and to the woman behind Royce Dugan. Whenever he glanced over his shoulder, Charlie Blunt was always staring at him. He wished he could read her mind. Wearing a dress and with her hair in a bun, she seemed so prim and innocent, not the same woman who had attacked her dead father so viciously. He found himself strangely attracted to her in spite of the risk she posed for him.

Her gaze discomforted him and he stared often out the window behind the jury box. He studied the thick tree branch just outside as it swayed gently under its own weight. It would hold him, if he could reach it. As the jury box filled, he gauged his ability to crash through the men, dive out the window and catch the branch. With shackled hands, it would be a risk.

In addition to the men in the jury, Hampton knew he would have to get past the Texas Ranger Scott Lewis. Lewis had narrow, no-nonsense eyes that seemed to take in everything and everybody.

Hampton looked back over his shoulder and saw Charlie Blunt still staring at him. Beside her on one side sat Josie and on the other the Lazy B hands Cyrus McCurdy, Ivey Yates, Olean Evans and Bibb Aultrong. The four would likely testify however Dugan had told them to, but their testimony would carry little weight compared to what Charlie and Josie Blunt said — particularly if they accused him of ravishing them.

Slowly the jury box grew crowded. Hampton recognized a few, but most were strangers. They sat with solemn faces and eyes that too frequently gazed at him. As the morning dragged by, hunger gnawed fiercely at Hampton's stomach. His daydream of charging for the window and escaping down the tree provided a pleasant diversion from the proceedings but could not subdue the hunger in his stomach. He had gone three mealtimes without food, save for the candy thrown through his window.

When the final seat in the jury box was occupied, Spencer Yantis pulled a pocket watch from his vest and noted the time. As the judge explained to the jury its responsibilities, Yantis leaned over to Hampton. "I don't know that they're impartial, but they were the best I could do. I hope they're smart enough to see where I'm leading them."

Hampton nodded absently, more concerned with filling the pit in his growling stomach. "Do we get lunch? The sheriff hasn't fed me in three meals."

Anger flared in Yantis's eyes. "He what?"

"After the judge visited my cell and ordered him to give me a spoon at the meals, that's all I've gotten from him. No food, just a spoon. The sheriff's laughed about it. Somebody tossed me some candy through the window last night, or I'd have had nothing to eat. Was that you?"

"No," Yantis said, turning around to study the crowd. "Where's the sheriff?"

Hampton lifted his shackled hand and pointed at Perry Johns, sitting on the ledge of a back window. Several spectators craned their necks to see the target of Hampton's finger.

"Good," Yantis said, straightening in his chair as the judge finished lecturing the jury men on their responsibility under the law and as guardians of the accused's life and liberty. "It's a quarter after noon, Hugh; we should be breaking for lunch soon."

The judge stared down from his bench at the lawyers and Hampton. "Gentlemen, if you have no additional business, I suggest we recess for lunch and reconvene in one hour. Is that acceptable?"

"Yes, Your Honor," replied Yantis, arising from his chair, "if I might ask one final question."

The judge nodded. "Go ahead, Mr. Yantis."

"Does the defendant get a meal?"

The judge cocked his head and stared over the top of his reading glasses at Yantis. "Why, yes, but why do you ask?"

"Your Honor, my client informs me that since you inspected his jail cell yesterday and instructed Sheriff Johns to provide him a spoon for his meals, that is all the sheriff has provided. No food."

The judge jerked his reading glasses off his nose and scanned the room. "Sheriff Johns?"

"Back here, Judge," the sheriff said, sliding from the window ledge to his feet and squeezing through the crowd toward the aisle.

"Is that the truth?"

"What, Judge? I was having trouble hearing."

"That you haven't fed the prisoner a meal since breakfast yesterday morning."

The sheriff stumbled over his words. "It's, we've . . ." He shook his head. "I can't say. It's my deputy's job to feed him."

"Sheriff, I'm making it your job now. See that he's fed and fed well at every meal. I will hold you in contempt of court if you disobey."

The sheriff nodded.

The judge stared and raised his eyebrows. "I didn't hear you."

The sheriff nodded again.

"Sheriff, since I'm having great trouble hearing your assurance that the prisoner will be fed in an appropriate manner, I am hereby ordering you to bring meals for him, his attorney and Rangers Lewis and Michael to the courtroom during our noon recess. In this manner I shall be able to observe firsthand that you have obeyed my orders. Understood?"

"Yes, sir," the sheriff responded.

The judge nodded. "Good. Now then, ladies and gentlemen, after I call for a lunch recess you will be required to leave the courtroom, all except the defendant, his lawyer and the Rangers. Any men who want their weapons on the way out can have them, but they will not be allowed back in the courtroom this afternoon."

Several men groaned.

Taking his gavel, the judge rapped it against the bench. "Order in the court, order in the court." Williams waited until silence prevailed before speaking again. "This will expedite the punctual resumption of the trial." He banged the gavel one more time and picked up his revolver from the high bench. "If the jury will follow me, these proceedings will resume in one hour. Court is recessed." He led the jury out the back door as the room exploded with conversation and laughter.

Hampton stood up, stretching his legs and walking around the table. "Good job, Spencer, good job."

Yantis shook his head. "Wait until the job is over before offering any congratulations. You might not feel so good then."

The courtroom was jumbled with many people trying to squeeze out for lunch, some trying to visit with friends and others making their way to the front.

Hampton saw the sheriff approaching the railing, going against the tide of people exiting for lunch. The sheriff caught Dugan's attention, but the attorney scowled.

"You better be finding four lunches like the judge said."

"But . . ." shot back the sheriff.

"But, hell, Sheriff," Dugan challenged. "You're gonna ruin a good case if you don't quit twisting the judge's tail."

The sheriff threw up his hands and turned around, inching toward the door with the crowd.

Hampton saw Let and Matilda Gibson approaching the railing. The moment Let reached across the bar to shake Hampton's hand, the Ranger Scott Lewis was beside the defendant, eyeing Gibson closely. Let withdrew his hand and Lewis nodded his approval.

"We're behind you, Hugh."

"Thank you," Hampton replied. "Are you the ones that sent me the horehound candy?"

Let looked at Matilda and both shook their heads. "When the time's right," Let said, "we'll get you whatever you need." He stared for a moment at the Ranger, then grabbed Matilda's arm and tugged her toward the door.

Claude Stanley approached, a smile on his face. "Things'll work out for you. Decent folks know you didn't have anything to do with all these crimes."

Hampton nodded. "I appreciate your comments and thank you for the suit of clothes."

Stanley grinned. "The cattle you left me to settle up your account more than covered the suit."

"Did you send the candy?"

The store owner shrugged. "What candy?"

Hampton shook his head. "Candy sent to me in jail. Have you sold much horehound candy in the last day or two?"

Stanley frowned. "Much as I hate to admit it, Charlie Blunt's the only one that's bought any horehound candy from me. Maybe some of the clerks have sold some. Charlie likes it, though, because I saw her eating a few pieces earlier."

The Ranger Lewis motioned for Stanley to join the stragglers exiting the courtroom. The merchant obliged. All the spectators except one were clumped at the door, slowly moving out into the hall. Charlie Blunt remained seated, her glance alternating between Hampton and Royce Dugan, who gathered his papers at his table.

Hampton had the feeling she was lingering to say something, perhaps to him or perhaps to Dugan.

As the other spectators crowded into the hall, Ranger Michael at the back closed the door. "Ma'am," Michael called across the room, "you need to leave like the others."

Dugan glanced around to see whom the Ranger had addressed. "Oh, Charlie, just a minute and I'll see you out."

Hampton saw her jaw tighten for a moment, then she stood up wordlessly but gracefully and retreated down the aisle, ignoring Dugan's call. The prosecutor shook his head, finished gathering his materials, then left the courtroom.

Ranger Michael locked the courtroom door behind him, then marched to join Lewis at Hampton's side.

"See any that looked like troublemakers, Jason?" Lewis asked as he walked over to the jury box.

"The sheriff," Michael replied with a hollow laugh.

Lewis entered the jury box and marched to the middle of the back row. He propped his Winchester against the wall, then leaned on a chair and reached for the bottom of the open window. He tugged it down and latched it.

After retrieving his rifle, Lewis addressed Michael but looked at Hampton. "Jason, did you notice how close that tree branch comes to the window?"

"Didn't notice it, Scott; do you think

anybody else did?"

Lewis stared at Hampton. "I'd hate to think so."

Hampton couldn't help but nod to Lewis. The Ranger had put him on notice not to try anything. "Will it bother you if I walk around?" Hampton asked.

Lewis shook his head. "Not as long as you stay away from the jury box."

Yantis took Hampton's arm and turned to Lewis. "Mind if we step up to the judge's bench for a private conversation between lawyer and client?"

Michael pointed at Lewis. "The judge took his six-shooter, didn't he?"

Lewis nodded at Michael, then spoke to Yantis. "Go ahead."

The lawyer pulled Hampton to the bench. "Hugh," he whispered, "I want to make sure you won't try to escape. It'd only hurt my chances of getting you off."

"I haven't stopped thinking about it since I was jailed."

"Don't do anything foolish yet. If I think we can't win, I'll let you know. Things are going well. The sheriff may have his thumb over Brown County, but he doesn't control the judge. I think we'll win for sure if Dugan calls all four of the Blunt men. Did you see that one that lifted his hand when I asked where Simon Levine's body might be buried?"

A grin crossed Hampton's face. "I thought I was the only one who saw it."

"If Dugan puts him on the stand, I can rattle him and maybe even get him to admit Blunt killed Levine."

At the back of the courtroom, Hampton heard a knock on the door and then a curse in a voice Hampton recognized. It was the sheriff and lunch.

Michael retreated down the aisle and unlocked the door. The sheriff and his deputy entered, both carrying a plate in each hand. They took them to the defense table and left them there. The sheriff took eating utensils out of his pocket and made a show of placing a spoon, fork and knife at each place before spinning around and leaving, the deputy on his tail.

Yantis called out after Johns. "Thank you, Sheriff. If you hurry, you might be able to grab a bite and get back before you're declared in contempt of court." Johns grumbled and slammed the door behind him, the Ranger Michael locking it again.

Hampton licked his lips at the sight of fried chicken, creamed potatoes, gravy, canned tomatoes and a hunk of cornbread.

Yantis took the cornbread from his plate

and shoved the remainder to Hampton. "You need it more than I do."

Hampton didn't argue. He sat down at the table and gobbled down his food, enjoying every bite of it. When he was finished with both plates, he gathered the tinware along with the empties of Lewis and Michael. "Like me to take these outside?"

Lewis tossed Hampton a sly grin. "Good try, but I think I'll have the sheriff clear the dishes when he returns."

The four men laughed.

20

Looking down from his bench, Judge Gregory Williams stared into quiet submission the spectators crowded like cattle in the sweltering courtroom. Then he nodded at Royce Dugan. "Would the state call its first witness?"

The county attorney stood up and strutted before the judge's bench, staring all the time at Hugh Hampton. "The state calls Mr. Ivey Yates."

Yates arose, grinning at his companions in the front row as he squeezed past them to the aisle. He approached the witness stand with his thumbs hooked in the empty holster on each hip. After he was sworn in, Yates took his seat, crossed his arms over his chest and smirked at Hampton.

The lawyer Yantis leaned over to Hampton. "Now the fun begins."

Dugan asked Yates to describe what he saw the evening that Lemuel Blunt was murdered.

Yates nodded. "We had just finished eating supper and had stepped outside on the porch to have a smoke when Lem decided it was time for his evening ride."

"Why'd he go on a ride each night?"

"He circled the place, making sure everything was in order."

"Any other reason?" Dugan asked.

Yates's brow narrowed with hesitation for a moment. "He feared Hampton was going to try to assassinate him."

Yantis shot up from his chair. "Objection."

"Objection overruled."

Slowly, Yantis sank back in his chair.

Dugan cleared his throat. "Thank you, Your Honor. Now describe what happened, Mr. Yates."

"The rest of us was sitting on the porch when we hear two gunshots. We jump up and see him come up the rise, waving his hat and yelling for help."

"And then what happened?"

Yates nodded. "We jumped for our horses and all raced out to help him."

"Did you see your boss killed?"

"Yes, sir, I did."

Dugan stroked his chin. "Is the man who killed him in this room?"

Lifting his finger, Yates pointed at Hampton. "That's him . . . Hugh Hampton."

"Thank you, Mr. Yates," Dugan said. "I have no further questions."

Yantis stood up slowly, licked his lips and approached the witness stand.

Yates squirmed in his seat.

"Now, Mr. Yates," the defense lawyer began, "how far is it from the ranch house where you were to the spot where Lem Blunt died?"

"A quarter-mile."

"And your eyesight is so good that you can state without fear of error he was killed by Mr. Hampton?"

He nodded.

"The court cannot hear you," the judge said.

"My eyes are plenty good enough for that. I saw Hampton murder Lem."

"Now, Mr. Yates, you said you saw Blunt come up the rise and wave his hat for help."

"That's right."

"Well, sir, if he had to come up the rise for help, how could you see Mr. Hampton or anyone else?"

Yates glanced from Yantis to Dugan, then looked at the floor in front of the witness stand.

"I'm awaiting an answer; the jury that will decide Mr. Hampton's fate is awaiting an answer. Your eyesight's not so good that you can see through the ground, is it?"

"No, dammit, but we rode out to help; that's when I saw Lem killed by Hampton."

"Who's we, Mr. Yates? Who rode out with you and saw Blunt killed?"

"Me and the other hands."

"Name them."

Yates cocked his head. "They was Cyrus McCurdy, Olean Evans and Bibb Aultrong."

"That's all?"

"Yep." Yates nodded.

Yantis turned around and strode toward the jury box, bending over and placing his hands firmly on the railing and staring at the jurors. When he asked the next question, he looked at the jury, not at Yates.

"Now, Mr. Yates, there have been some vicious rumors circulated that once my client supposedly murdered Lemuel Blunt, he then proceeded to ravish the victim's daughters. How did Mr. Hampton supposedly commit this crime if the young women stayed at the house? How could my client have murdered Blunt, apparently fought off you and the others and still found time to humiliate the women?"

"Objection," shouted Dugan, shoving himself up from his table. "The state has not pressed any charges for rape. The question is immaterial."

"Your Honor," countered Yantis, spinning around from the jury box, "the lies told against my client are so numerous that I cannot defend him without tripping over the falsehoods."

Judge Williams dropped his head and stared over the top of his glasses at the defense attorney. "I will sustain the state's objection, sir, since the state has not made any accusation of rape before me."

Yantis dropped his head and nodded. "As you wish, Your Honor, but may I have a moment to confer with my client?"

"Granted," said the judge.

A somber expression on his face, Yantis approached Hampton, then bent and whispered in his ear. "That's what I wanted. It will make Dugan think twice before bringing up a rape allegation in this proceeding."

Hampton nodded and patted Yantis on the shoulder. The lawyer straightened, shook his head and pinched the bridge of his nose before approaching Yates again.

"Now, Mr. Yates," the lawyer resumed, "did the women ride with you?"

"Yes, yes," he nodded, "I forgot about them."

"Thank you. Now did the women saddle

up horses while you waited?"

Yates grinned. "Charlie caught her pa's horse and Josie . . ."

Yantis smiled. "Charlie Blunt rode her pa's horse? How could that be?"

A wide grin broke across Yates's face. "She stuck her foot in the stirrup and pulled herself aboard."

The spectators laughed and the judge instantly gaveled the room to order.

"You make fun of the situation, Mr. Yates, but do you understand the concept of perjury?"

Yates looked at the jury box. "Perjury?"

"Yes, Mr. Yates, that's the crime of telling a lie while you are under an oath."

"I ain't lied."

"Then why, Mr. Yates, do you at one point say that you saw Hugh Hampton kill Lem Blunt, yet on the other hand admit that his daughter caught Blunt's own horse before she rode out with you to help? Was Blunt still in the saddle?"

"No!"

"The fact is," Yantis said, pointing his finger at Yates's nose, "you don't know what happened below the rise. Nor do any of the other men who rode with you. You were all too late and too cowardly to know what happened."

"Objection," shouted Dugan.

"Sustained," responded the judge. "Members of the jury, disregard the last comment by Mr. Yantis."

"No further questions," Yantis replied, marching to his table. He sat down and crossed his arms confidently over his chest.

Yates stepped down from the witness stand and stomped past Yantis. "Bastard," he mumbled.

"Mr. Yates," Judge Williams shouted, "that language is inappropriate for a court of law."

"Bastard," Yates said defiantly.

Williams slammed the gavel. "Sheriff, arrest this man for contempt of court and put him in jail until otherwise ordered."

Sheriff Perry Johns grimaced, but acquiesced. "Yes, sir," he said to the judge, then he motioned to Yates. "Come with me, Ivey."

The hand looked bewildered as the sheriff led him past the Ranger at the back door.

The judge turned to Dugan. "Next witness."

Dugan seemed less confident than he had when he called Ivey Yates to the stand. "The state calls Cyrus McCurdy to testify."

McCurdy swaggered up to the witness stand, a snarl on his face as he studied Yantis and Hampton. After he was sworn in, McCurdy slouched into the chair and stared at Royce Dugan.

Hampton thought Yantis was succeeding in planting doubts in Dugan's mind, but wondered if the jury had the same reservations. Dugan covered basically the same ground with McCurdy that he had with Yates, then turned the questioning over to Yantis.

The lawyer stood up and loosened his tie. "It's warm in here, isn't it? Maybe as hot as the fire that burned down my client's cabin."

"Yeah," McCurdy smirked, then paused, realizing what he had said. "Yeah, it's hot in here. I wouldn't know anything about his cabin fire."

"Objection," called Dugan. "Counselor should get on with the questioning, not the idle talk."

"Sustained," said the judge. "Please continue with a line of questioning more germane to the issue at hand, Mr. Yantis."

"Yes, Your Honor," Yantis said, pacing back and forth between the witness stand and the jury box. "Now, Mr. McCurdy, where were you when Lem Blunt was shot?"

"On the porch with everyone else."

"Did you see him get shot?"

"I did."

"What did you see?"

"We heard a couple shots and he rode up

the rise, Blunt did, and waved his hat for help. Then Hampton shot him, knocked him out of the saddle. The horse stampeded back to the house, that's how Charlie caught him. Then we all rode out to help him, if we could."

Yantis ran his fingers through his hair and shook his head. "Hugh Hampton shot him, you're sure?"

"Sure as I'm sitting here."

"Well, Mr. McCurdy, what I don't understand is this: Whoever shot Lem Blunt apparently hid below the rise so he couldn't be seen from the house, yet you and Mr. Yates were able to see him. How do you explain that?"

"We saw Hampton when we rode to help Lem."

Yantis nodded. "Big difference, though, in seeing him then and seeing him kill Lemuel Blunt. If you are stating the truth . . ."

"I am, dammit," he flared, drawing an instant admonition from the judge.

"Another outburst of that type and you will be held in contempt of court and jailed," Williams said. "Continue, Mr. Yantis."

"If you are stating the truth, you were able to see from a quarter of a mile away that Mr. Hampton fired the fatal shot. Is that

263

correct."

"That's what I saw," he answered, shrugging at Dugan.

Yantis turned to the jury. "At a quarter-of-a-mile distance, you are able to say with absolute certainty you saw who killed Lemuel Blunt, even though the assassin had taken up a position out of sight of the porch. I am amazed at your keen powers of observation, Mr. McCurdy. Now then, Mr. McCurdy, since I've explained the concept of perjury to Mr. Yates, I'm sure you don't need another explanation — because of your keen powers of observation. However, I wonder if you understand the concept of self-defense. Do you?"

McCurdy nodded emphatically. "A man can protect himself when someone else attacks him."

"Very good, Mr. McCurdy," Yantis began.

McCurdy cocked his head and nodded his surprise.

Yantis continued. "A man can protect himself when someone else attacks him or his property. Would that be a fair statement of your definition?"

"It would."

"Then Lemuel Blunt would have been justified in shooting at his attacker?"

"He would."

"Now say his attacker fired, but Lemuel Blunt waited a bit to return the fire. How long would it be reasonable for a man to wait to defend himself and his property? A minute, five minutes, an hour, a day, a week?"

"As long as it took to protect himself," McCurdy replied.

"Well, if Lemuel Blunt's killer, whoever he was, had burned down Lemuel Blunt's house, would Lemuel Blunt have been justified in defending his life or property against future attacks?"

"I guess," replied McCurdy, the cockiness evaporating from his face as the line of questioning began to trouble him.

"Let's assume then, Mr. McCurdy, that Mr. Hampton, the defendant, was indeed the killer."

"Easy to assume, because he was," McCurdy replied.

"Because you saw him?"

"That's right."

"Well, good, Mr. McCurdy, because the defendant is prepared to take the stand and testify that he saw you and Lemuel Blunt in the light of his burning house, the house that you helped blow up."

"Objection," shouted Dugan, jumping to

his feet. "This is not a trial of Mr. Mc-Curdy."

"He didn't see me there," McCurdy cried out, then seemed to feel he had incriminated himself, ". . . because I wasn't there."

"Objection, objection, objection," Dugan shouted in an attempt to silence McCurdy.

"Your Honor," pleaded Yantis, "this is but one thread of many lies that the state is trying to wrap into a noose around my client's neck."

"Sustained," replied the judge. "Jury is instructed to disregard the last comment. Proceed."

Yantis nodded. "As you wish, Your Honor." Yantis paced to the jury box, looking at the stone-faced and sweaty men, several of them fanning their hats at their faces. "Had Lemuel Blunt ever threatened Hugh Hampton?"

McCurdy shrugged. "Lem was a tough man. Maybe he did, maybe he didn't."

"Did Lemuel Blunt blow up Hugh Hampton's place or the Gillyard brothers'?"

"Objection," Dugan said.

Yantis exploded across the room toward the bench and the judge. "My client did not murder Lemuel Blunt, but if the jury will not believe that, I want them to at least understand he felt threatened by Blunt, as did all the small ranchers across Pecan Creek."

Judge Williams banged the gavel against the bench. "Order," he demanded, then pointed the gavel at Yantis. "You will contain your outbursts or be held in contempt of court. The court will overrule the objection, sir, but not because of your outburst. This court will decide on issues of law and will not be influenced by emotion."

His face taut with anger, Yantis spun around toward Hampton. "Yes, Your Honor," he replied, then took a couple slow, calming breaths. Slowly, he faced the jury, staring intently at them before addressing McCurdy again. "We are awaiting your answer, Mr. McCurdy. Did Lemuel Blunt blow up Hugh Hampton's place or kill the Gillyard brothers?"

McCurdy's lips twisted into a snarl. "He did not."

"What about you and the other hands, McCurdy? Did you blow up his cabin?"

"Hell, no," shot back McCurdy, "we're just cowhands doing our job, trying to save as many cattle as we could during the drought."

Yantis shook his head slowly, deliberately. "Wasn't your job really to drive off the small ranchers so Lemuel Blunt could get their land and what little water they had?"

"Objection," called Dugan. "The issue is who killed Lem Blunt, not what his men were supposed to do."

"Sustained," the judge said.

Yantis lowered his head and strode back to his seat. "No further questions," he said as he slid into his chair beside his client.

Hampton thought he saw a glimmer of defeat in Yantis's eyes, and he glanced at the sturdy branch of the pecan tree within reach of the window behind the jurors. As he looked away, he saw the Ranger Scott Lewis, his Winchester cradled in his arm, nodding slightly, as if he could read Hampton's thoughts.

Leaning over to Yantis, Hampton whispered. "Is the judge against us, too?"

Yantis shrugged. "He's going by the book. He won't do us any favors, but he won't show any to the prosecutor, either."

"It doesn't look good now, does it?"

Yantis stroked his chin, then wadded his fingers into a fist, which he dropped atop the papers before him. "We're holding our own, nothing more. I'll rattle the next two hands, particularly Bibb Aultrong, and raise some reasonable doubts, but these men don't worry me. It's Charlie and Josie who can hang you."

Hampton nodded, then watched the prosecutor stand up.

Dugan grabbed both lapels of his coat and addressed the judge. "Your Honor, in light of the untruthful implications the defense has showered upon the reputation of the late Lemuel Blunt, I should like to call to the stand the sheriff of Brown County, Perry Johns."

"Damn," whispered Yantis, his knotted fist hitting the table, "this means Dugan won't call Evans or Aultrong. He cut me off at the knees."

Hampton glanced out the window at the tree branch. It might be his only chance at justice if Spencer Yantis and the law let him down.

21

After taking the oath, Sheriff Perry Johns folded his lanky frame in the witness chair and gazed across the spectators like a king before his subjects. As bad a man as Lemuel Blunt had been, Hugh Hampton thought him at least a hair better than the sheriff. Blunt had broken the law, of course, but he made no pretenses of respecting any rule but that of his own needs or wants. The sheriff, meanwhile, wore a lawman's badge while protecting the lawless. That was the worse sin.

The sheriff leaned back in his chair and cast a haughty gaze toward Hampton.

"Now, Sheriff," said Royce Dugan, strutting before the jury box, "I had not planned to have you take the stand, the testimony of Ivey Yates and Cyrus McCurdy being sufficient in my mind to convict Hugh Hampton for the cowardly murder of one of Brown County's most respected citizens.

However, the defense has brought up accusations that Lemuel Blunt bombed the Gillyard brothers, then bombed Hugh Hampton's place as well, groundless accusations that I would like to refute."

The sheriff shifted in his seat, a knowing smile creasing his slender face.

Dugan crossed his arms over his chest. "Do you believe Lemuel Blunt or any of his men bombed the Gillyard place?"

Johns stared at Hampton as he answered. "No, sir, I do not."

"Explain why," responded the prosecutor.

Johns nodded slowly. "I think Hugh Hampton assassinated the Gillyards."

The courtroom erupted in surprise, Judge Gregory Williams gaveling it to order.

"Objection," called Yantis, shooting up from his chair.

Hampton tugged at the lawyer's sleeve. "It's lies, all of it."

The lawyer shrugged. "What isn't?"

"Order, order," called the judge.

Hampton looked at the crowd, spotting Spud Davis, Johnny Walls and Let Gibson, who sat with his wife, shaking his head and biting his lips. Beyond them, at the back of the room, Hampton noted the Ranger Jason Michael alertly watching everyone for any sign of trouble.

"Objection," shouted Yantis above the din. "This is speculation, nothing more."

The judge pounded the gavel. "Order, or I'll clear the courtroom." Slowly the room began to calm.

"Your Honor," called prosecutor Dugan, "the defense accused the deceased, a man who is no longer here to defend his good name, of an insidious crime. I am only responding to his lead."

Judge Williams looked from Dugan to Yantis. "Objection overruled."

"But Your Honor . . ." protested Yantis.

The judge shook his head at Yantis. "Go ahead, Mr. Dugan."

"Thank you, Your Honor." Dugan turned to the sheriff. "Now, what led you to this conclusion?"

Sheriff Johns straightened in his chair. "Hugh Hampton came to town to report the bombing, but he already was pointing blame at Lem Blunt and his men. Anytime someone reports a killing and is pointing a finger at someone else, I always suspect whoever's doing the pointing."

Dugan nodded. "But surely, Sheriff, a man of your experience is basing this accusation on more than just your suspicions."

"Yes, sir." Johns nodded. "I accompanied him back to the Gillyard place. It was the night after a storm and I tried to convince him it had been lightning and a cyclone that had demolished the house, but he insisted it was dynamited. That got me to wondering if he might not have planted explosives."

The prosecutor clucked his tongue. "But Sheriff, with all due respect to you and your years of experience, that's still not proof in a court of law." Dugan marched to his table, then turned around to face Johns.

"I found tracks leading from Hampton's place to the Gillyard place, and then when I arrested Hampton, I found a stick of dynamite in his saddlebags — that and the Gillyards' Bible," Johns said.

The spectators took to murmuring for a moment, until Judge Williams pounded his gavel against the bench.

Yantis leaned over to Hampton. "That true about the dynamite in the saddlebag?"

Hampton nodded. "Found it after the unsuccessful attempt to blow up my cabin."

Yantis shook his head. "Dugan's digging us a big hole to crawl out of."

Dugan stepped away from his table and marched in front of Hampton, turning to stare at the defendant. "Is it true, Sheriff," continued the prosecutor, still focusing on Hampton, "that Hugh Hampton tried to show you tracks leading from the Gillyard place to Lemuel Blunt's?"

"It is, though I didn't see any tracks other than from his own horse. I figure he'd ridden over to blow up the Blunt place and got scared away."

Yantis bounced up from his chair. "Objection, Your Honor, that is pure speculation."

Dugan bounded toward the bench.

"Objection sustained," Williams intoned. "The jury should disregard the last response."

"Thank you, Your Honor," Yantis said, sitting down, then leaning over to Hampton. "There were tracks, were there not?"

Hampton nodded.

"You followed them with the sheriff, did you not, to the Blunt place?"

Again Hampton nodded.

"Did the sheriff do anything when you made the accusation?"

"Nope," Hampton replied. "I left alone and the sheriff was invited to stay and take a poke at one of Blunt's daughters."

Yantis flinched and stared doubly hard at Hampton. "Then Lem Blunt let the sheriff sleep with one of his daughters."

Hampton shrugged. "We've all heard the stories about how Lemuel Blunt used his daughters."

A sly smile flicked across Yantis's face as

Dugan ended his examination of the sheriff.

"Your witness," Dugan said as he took his seat.

Yantis exploded from his chair and strode straight for the witness stand, stopping not three feet from the sheriff's face.

"Did you go with Hugh Hampton to the Gillyard place after it was demolished?"

"Sure did," Johns said, crossing his arms over his chest.

"And from there you went to the Blunt place?"

Johns nodded.

"Why?"

"It was my job to check out all the possibilities."

"There were no tracks to the Blunt place — or at least that's what you've testified. You've also testified you thought it was a cyclone and lightning that destroyed the place. If there were no tracks and you thought the place was destroyed by a bad cloud, why did you go to the Lazy B?"

"Hugh Hampton made a serious allegation I needed to check out."

"Was that the reason, Sheriff, or was there something else?"

"Huh?"

"Did you have carnal relations with one of Lemuel Blunt's daughters?"

"Have what?"

"Objection," Dugan shouted, jumping up from his chair.

"Sustained," shouted the judge.

Yantis ignored the judge and leaned closer to the sheriff's face. "Did you bed down one of his daughters?" Yantis yelled.

"You son of a bitch," cried Johns, his face turning red.

The judge pounded the bench with his gavel. "That question was overruled, Mr. Yantis. Any more willful disobedience of this court's rulings will see you jailed for contempt charges. Understand?"

Yantis nodded slowly. "Yes, Your Honor."

Hampton glanced from the judge to Charlie Blunt and her sister in the front row. Josie seemed defiant, her chin thrust in the air, but Charlie hung her head.

"Now," the judge chided, "the jury will disregard the last statement, and you may resume questions as long as they are germane to the issue at hand."

Yantis backed away from the witness stand. "Now Sheriff, if Hugh Hampton bombed the Gillyard place, then who bombed Hampton's cabin?"

Johns smirked. "Hugh Hampton did."

"His own place, Sheriff? Why?"

"He knew I was getting close to fingering

him for the Gillyard murders. He was trying to throw me off his tail."

Yantis shook his head. "Seems he might've blown up his barn, but not his cabin and all his belongings."

Johns cocked his head confidently. "He knew I would get him."

Yantis shook his head. "No, sir, he knew you were wrong. He knew you were in bed with Blunt . . ." Yantis paused and stepped toward the bench, a sly smile flicking across his lips. "I apologize, Your Honor, for such a poor choice of words as 'in bed with Blunt' in light of my previous allegation's having been overruled by this wise court."

Judge Williams wiped the perspiration from his forehead, a slight grin crossing his face. "Had that not been an accident and had you not corrected yourself, Mr. Yantis, I would've been forced to hold you in contempt."

Yantis nodded. "Again, my apologies." He retreated toward Hugh Hampton. "No further questions, Your Honor."

As the sheriff stepped down from the witness stand, Royce Dugan stood up and announced his next witness. "The state calls Charlie Blunt."

Instantly, Spencer Yantis turned around. "Your Honor," he called, "might I suggest we recess until tomorrow morning. There are matters I must discuss with the defendant. And, the afternoon heat is stifling in this cramped courtroom, a danger indeed to the fine citizens of Brown County who have seen fit to observe justice served."

The judge seemed to hesitate.

"And surely, Your Honor, this has been a trying day for Miss Charlie Blunt, with all the testimony about her father's unfortunate death."

Judge Williams looked at the prosecutor. "Do you have any objections?"

"No, sir, Your Honor. I can prove Hugh Hampton guilty of Lem Blunt's murder in the heat of the afternoon or the cool of the morning."

The judge nodded. "Very well, then; but before court is adjourned, I shall instruct Ranger Scott Lewis to return the prisoner to the jailhouse."

Lewis stepped forward and motioned for Hampton to rise.

As Hampton stood, Yantis grabbed his arm. "I'll visit you this evening and let you know my plans for tomorrow."

Hampton nodded, then followed the Texas Ranger down the aisle and out of the courtroom. Quickly, they marched down the hallway, then reached the stairs as the courtroom doors flew open, the people trying to escape the heat.

With Ranger Lewis beside him, he crossed the courthouse lawn and street so rapidly that few realized what had happened. Then he was inside the sheriff's office and back in his cell, the stone building cool in comparison to the sweltering courthouse.

At the opposite end of the cell block, Ivey Yates pranced like a caged animal in his cell. "When's someone gonna pay my bail?" he called as Ranger Lewis locked Hampton's cell, then departed.

Yates cursed Lewis, then turned his profanity on Hampton, who collapsed on his bunk and ignored him. Yates finally tired of spouting off unanswered taunts and sat on his cot, his elbows propped on his knees, his face in his hands.

Come suppertime, Sheriff Perry Johns himself carried in two plates and two spoons for his prisoners.

"When am I getting out?" Yates demanded of Perry.

"As soon as someone pays your twenty-dollar bail," Johns answered, shoving Yates's supper plate under the cell door.

"You've done us favors before," Yates said.

"Not with a judge in town, I haven't," he said, turning and walking toward Hampton.

At Hampton's cell, he tossed the spoon through the cell bars at Hampton, then bent and dropped the tin plate at the cell door. With the toe of his boot he shoved the plate into the cell.

Hampton never moved from his bed, just stared at the sheriff, studying him and wondering just how much he would enjoy killing Perry Johns.

"You bastard, telling your lawyer I slept with the Blunt girls," he snarled.

"True, wasn't it?" Hampton challenged.

Yates laughed. "Hell, we all took our pokes at Charlie and Josie, even Lem himself."

Hampton felt his stomach curdle.

The sheriff scowled at Hampton. "It'll satisfy me greatly to pull the trapdoor lever and watch you die at the end of a rope. I've hung men before, and most soil their britches. It's a damn funny thing to watch." He clanged the iron door shut behind him as he retreated into his office.

Hampton ignored the food and reclined on his cot, staring at the ceiling as the afternoon turned to evening and evening faded into night.

Hampton finally dozed off into a bored sleep, only to be disturbed by the sheriff's laugh at the door. Hampton shook his head and propped himself up on his cot as Perry

Johns opened the iron outer door and stepped into the room.

"Ivey Yates, you lucky son of a bitch, your bail's been paid by Hampton's lawyer. Ain't that funny?"

Hampton turned over and scratched his head.

Johns marched to Yates's cell and quickly unlocked the door. No sooner did he swing it open than Yates rushed out of the cell room and into the sheriff's office.

As he exited, Spencer Yantis walked in. "Sorry I'm late," he said.

"I didn't have any place to go," replied Hampton.

As Yantis marched by, the sheriff grabbed his arm. "I ain't gonna forget you saying I slept with the Blunt girls. Once Hampton is hung, I'll find some way to settle our score."

The sheriff released Yantis's arm and marched out of the room, slamming the iron door shut. Quickly, Hampton was on his feet and moving to the bars. He kicked the plate of supper out of the way. "Why'd you pay Yates's bail?"

Yantis said nothing until he stood opposite Hampton. "I couldn't risk anyone overhearing what I'm about to say," he answered softly. "Nothing I've done has worked, Hugh. I intend to see justice is served tomorrow, even if the law isn't. I was late getting here tonight because I met with Let Gibson, Johnny Walls and Spud Davis. They're going to sneak in weapons tomorrow. If the verdict comes back wrong, they'll help you escape."

Hampton whistled.

"I'll smuggle a pistol in my left boot, so you can get it. We'll have a good horse tied out near the pecan tree."

Hampton shook his head. "I don't know. I hate to drag more down with me."

"If Charlie Blunt tells as many lies as the previous witnesses, you won't stand a chance of receiving justice."

"I don't stand a chance as it is."

Yantis shrugged. "If we can get the drop on the Rangers, you might be able to escape. If we're lucky, there won't be any more killing. I wish there was another way, but if the verdict comes back guilty, then it's time to move. The others will be ready."

Hampton sighed. "Killing a Ranger's not something to look forward to."

"You may not have to," Yantis replied.

Hampton shook his head. "Ranger Lewis will not let me escape. I've seen the determination in his eyes."

Yantis shook Hampton's hand. "Who knows? I might come up with a bit of legal genius that will save my reputation and your neck"

Hampton nodded. "It's easier to live without a reputation than without a neck."

22

"The state of Texas calls Miss Charlie Blunt to testify," announced prosecutor Royce Dugan.

Charlie arose from the front row of spectators, where she sat with her sister, Ivey Yates, Olean Evans, Bibb Aultrong and Cyrus McCurdy. The four hands had cocky, confident demeanors as she made her way to the aisle and approached the witness stand. Beyond them stood Sheriff Perry Johns, a wide grin upon his narrow face.

As she passed the table where Hugh Hampton sat, her gaze met his for an instant. Her dark eyes were dangerous, yet alluring. No man could trust her and she could trust no man. Hampton watched the sway of her hips as she approached the witness stand. Her hair was pinned in a bun atop her head, and she was wearing the same dress she had worn the previous day. Hampton wondered if it was the only dress she owned.

After she was sworn in, she took a seat and crossed her hands in her lap. Very calmly she looked toward Dugan and the Lazy B hands behind him. Her gaze hardened. Hampton took a deep breath. This woman could hang him.

Twisting around to locate his allies, Hampton saw Johnny Walls and Spud Davis on opposite sides of the back row. Their job would be to disarm Jason Michael at the back. Hampton then nodded at Let Gibson, who sat in the row immediately behind him. Hampton was glad that neither Gibson nor Walls had brought their wives. If there was trouble, he didn't want to risk their injury.

Hampton straightened in his chair, glanced at the judge, then studied Ranger Scott Lewis, his back against the wall, his Winchester cradled in his arm. Hampton gauged his chances in a shoot-out with Lewis and didn't like them. Though Hampton didn't know how good Lewis was with a rifle, he was a Texas Ranger and that was good enough credentials to show he could take care of himself and any trouble he might encounter.

The lawyer Yantis scooted his chair closer to Hampton. "I won't be standing much today," Yantis whispered. "I fear my pants leg might get snagged by the pistol or someone might notice the bulge in my boot. Too, I don't want to appear intimidating to the Blunt women. It can work against us."

Hampton nodded as Royce Dugan moved slowly, respectfully, from his table toward the Witness.

"Miss Blunt," Dugan began, "I know this will be tough for you, but I know you want to see the man who killed your father put to the appropriate justice."

Charlie Blunt smiled weakly.

"Now" said Dugan, "did you see the murder?"

Charlie nodded. "Yes, sir. I was out riding with my sister after supper," she began.

Hampton turned to Yantis and whispered, "She's lying."

The lawyer nodded. "Good! Her testimony already conflicts with that of McCurdy and Yates. That ought to raise reasonable doubts in the jury's mind."

"So you could see the murder and who did it?"

"Oh, yes," she replied, "very plainly. Pa always kept a bottle of good liquor hidden among the rocks out of sight from the house. He liked to take an evening snort without the hands knowing it and without him having to share some expensive whiskey."

Dugan walked toward the jury. "And you and your sister were out riding when he was shot."

Charlie pursed her lips and nodded. "Yes."

Hampton could still see the aftermath of the killing vividly, both Charlie and Josie shooting their dead father's body, kicking him and spitting on him. The thought still made him shudder.

"Is the killer in the courtroom today?"

She nodded and looked toward Hampton, but her demeanor was strange. Hampton thought she had actually smiled at him for the briefest of instants.

"I know this will be hard on you," Dugan said, "but can you identify him for us?"

Charlie Blunt grimaced as if doubts had entered her mind. "Kind of," she replied.

Dugan blinked and seemed surprised by her answer. After a moment of silence, he spoke again. "Are you afraid?"

"Yes," she nodded, "because if I name names, I don't know what harm might come to me."

Dugan turned to the jury. "Gentlemen, this was such an insidious crime that even now a witness is scared to identify the murderer for fear of her own life." He turned back to Charlie Blunt. "The court and the state of Texas will protect you. Please, tell us who killed your father."

She nodded and spoke so softly that Hampton could not hear her.

"Please," soothed Dugan, "who killed your father?"

She sighed and stared straight at Dugan. "I can't say for certain because there was four of them."

Hampton gritted his teeth. The bitch! He leaned over, letting his shackled hand slide off the table toward Yantis's boot. He was ready to make his play. He would kill her to keep her from implicating Gibson, Walls and Davis, then make a break for the window, shooting it out with the Rangers.

Yantis, though, grabbed his hand and lifted it back on the table.

Hampton glanced around and saw Gibson, white-faced. Davis and Walls fidgeted at the back of the room.

Dugan, too, appeared for an instant, but seemed to catch his wits. "More than two dozen bullet wounds were found in Lemuel Blunt," he said. "It would make sense that more than one man was involved in the murder, but why haven't you spoken out before now?"

"I was scared they might kill me and my

sister like they did my pa."

Dugan crossed his arms over his chest and turned around and smiled. He stared at Hampton, then seemed to scan the audience for Gibson, Walls and Davis. "Why don't you go ahead and identify the murderers, starting with Hugh Hampton?"

Hampton tried again to reach for the gun in Yantis's boot.

"No," the lawyer said to Hampton, drawing a stern stare from the judge.

Charlie Blunt pointed straight at Hugh Hampton. "I can't start with him, because he didn't do it."

The crowd in the courtroom exploded into an excited clamor. The judge banged the gavel for order.

Hampton sighed, glad Yantis had prevented him from reaching his gun. Now, if only she wouldn't identify Gibson, Walls and Davis.

"Order, order," yelled Judge Williams, staring over the top of his glasses. "I'll not have this."

Dugan wilted like a dead vine and didn't seem to know what to do, but Charlie Blunt saved him the worry.

"The ones that killed my pa was his own hired hands, the same ones that have been violating me and my sister for years," she

289

screamed.

Instantly, Ivey Yates, Cyrus McCurdy and Olean Evans jumped to their feet, shouting and cursing. "Liar, liar," cried Yates. Slumped in his seat, Bibb Aultrong seemed too stunned to understand what had happened.

From the back of the room charged Ranger Jason Michael, signaling with his rifle for Blunt's hands to settle down.

"And," cried Charlie Blunt, "what the fancy lawyer said about the sheriff was true, too. He violated us many times."

Sheriff Perry Johns lunged toward the witness stand, his hand grabbing at his pistol.

The Ranger Scott Lewis intercepted him, shoving the point of his rifle in the sheriff's gut, then jerking Johns's pistol from his hand.

"Order, order," yelled the judge, banging the gavel against the bench to calm the commotion that had erupted.

"She's lying," shouted Royce Dugan to the judge.

The judge pointed his gavel at the prosecutor. "She's your witness."

"I move to drop charges," Dugan shouted back.

"Objection," yelled Spencer Yantis, bolting to his feet.

The judge slammed the gavel to the bench and stood up, his eyes flaring with anger. "Shut up, both of you," he said to the attorneys. Then he glowered at the spectators until a nervous hush, broken only by the curses of Blunt's hands and the sheriff, settled over the room. "Now, I will proceed with the questioning, Mr. Dugan, so take your seat. You, too, Mr. Yantis."

When the lawyers were seated, the judge settled back into his chair, then issued orders to the two Texas Rangers. "Keep watch on the men accused of crimes by Miss Blunt. If anyone makes a threatening gesture or move, shoot him."

A hush fell over the room.

"That's better," said Judge Williams, turning to Charlie Blunt.

"Now, Miss Blunt, please tell me what happened."

She nodded. "The four of them found out Pa had lied about how much money that Jew peddler had when they killed him. He held back money on them; that's what they believed. They got in an argument and the four of them killed him."

"It's a lie," shouted Yates.

Ranger Jason Michael slugged him across the side of the head with his rifle butt and he dropped to the floor.

"The sheriff was in on it, too."

"Liar," he called out, until Ranger Lewis shoved the rifle barrel hard into his stomach.

"They buried the peddler's body," Charlie continued, "and I can show you where."

The judge shook his head. "But why didn't you come forward before now?"

"They would've killed me like they did the peddler and the Gillyard brothers. They tried to kill Hugh Hampton, but couldn't."

The judge leaned closer to Charlie Blunt. "You're saying that Hugh Hampton was not present at the murder of your father. Is that right?"

Charlie nodded. "I didn't see him or anybody else except the four men that worked for my pa." She turned from the judge toward Hampton. "I didn't mean you no harm by not coming forward before now, but I was scared."

Hampton knew his face must be awash in disbelief. He tried to cover his shock as best he could, nodding slightly and turning to Spencer Yantis. "She's lying, Yantis," he whispered.

The lawyer nodded. "Perhaps justice will be served today, if not the law."

From the bench, the judge looked out over the spectators. "Miss Josie Blunt," he called, "please rise."

She stood, wide-eyed and trembling, biting her bottom lip. "Yes, sir," she said meekly.

"Would you agree now and later under oath to everything your sister has told this court?"

She nodded. "I will."

"Thank you, be seated." The judge sighed and looked down from the bench to Hugh Hampton. "Because of the nature of the testimony, I am ordering that all charges be dropped against Hugh Hampton."

"Objection," cried Spencer Yantis, standing up slowly from his seat.

Hampton glanced up, as bewildered by Yantis's actions as by Charlie Blunt's perjury on the witness stand.

"Your Honor," explained Yantis, "I request that this issue be turned over to the jury."

"That's superfluous, Mr. Yantis."

Yantis shook his head. "No, sir, in this case it is not. Charges that are dropped can be refiled. A man who has stood before a jury of his peers and been acquitted will never have to face such charges again."

The judge nodded. "Very well, if the formality will please you."

"Not me, Your Honor, but my client, who has been through an ordeal no innocent man should ever have to face twice."

Turning to the jury, the judge issued instructions. "The jury is to convene in my quarters for deliberations and return within five minutes with the appropriate verdict."

The jury arose and marched single file through the door behind the judge. No sooner had the door shut than Judge Williams issued orders to the Texas Rangers.

"Remove the badge from the sheriff and escort him and the other four accused to jail. One of you maintain guard over the prisoners and the other follow directions from Miss Charlie Blunt to the grave of the peddler. Report back to me as quickly as possible."

Rangers Scott Lewis and Jason Michael nodded. Lewis jerked the badge from Perry Johns's shirt and Michael herded his four prisoners toward the courtroom door. As they exited, the jury returned and marched back to their places.

"Has the jury reached a verdict?" asked the judge.

"We have," said the foreman, standing up. "We find the defendant not guilty."

A cheer arose from the spectators, drawing a final admonishment from the judge. "This court will remain orderly until adjournment." With that, the judge banged the gavel against the bench. "Court is adjourned."

An unrestrained cheer arose and Let Gibson was first to reach Hampton, slapping him on the back. "Can you believe it, can you believe it? It's over and you're free, in spite of a crooked sheriff and prosecutor."

"He had a good lawyer," Yantis laughed as he joined the celebration and congratulations.

Hampton slapped Yantis on the shoulder. The mirth, though, died quickly, and Hampton turned around to see what was the matter. On the opposite side of the table from him stood Charlie Blunt. She smiled slightly and nodded, seemingly embarrassed by the stares of so many.

Hampton smiled. "Thank you." He extended her his hand.

"No," she replied, "thank you." She took his hand by the wrist and turned it palm up. Then she placed something in it and pressed his fingers around it. She said nothing more, but moved to her sister and escorted her out of the court room.

Hampton watched the crowd part for the two women, and when the sisters had disappeared out the door, he opened his hand.

In his palm he held a piece of horehound candy.

23

The shrill whistle startled Hugh Hampton as he lifted his ax over his head. He glanced up from the log he was shaping to add to the wall of the new cabin and saw Charlie Blunt crossing the dry creek bed astride a bay mare. He had not seen her in the three weeks since the end of the trial, and she had reverted to her old form, wearing men's denim britches and a baggy workshirt knotted at the waist. But even the loose-fitting clothes could not hide all the curves of her body.

Hampton swung the ax toward the log and the steel blade thudded into the wood. Much had changed in the three weeks since she had deposited the piece of horehound candy in his hand and strode with her sister out of the courtroom. In that time, Hampton had repaired his corral and had built a modest shed that served as a barn and a place to throw his bed until he finished his new cabin. Now he went about his work without fear of ambush because justice, even if tainted by Charlie Blunt's perjury, had been quickly served by Judge Gregory Williams in a second trial. Sheriff Perry Johns had been sentenced to prison along with Olean Evans and Bibb Aultrong. Cyrus McCurdy and Ivey Yates had been sentenced to hang, based on the subsequent testimony of both Charlie and Josie Blunt. And Royce Dugan had fled Brown County. Hampton found himself remembering the lawyer Yantis's admonition that it is more important to serve justice than to serve the law.

Justice had been served and everything had changed, everything except the drought. But Hampton looked with anticipation to the west, where a long bank of clouds was building. The clouds held the hint of rain. Hampton lifted his hat and wiped the perspiration from his head as Charlie Blunt rode around the blackened heap of debris that had been his cabin.

Her smile, like her bearing, was tentative as she reined up the mare by the waist-high walls of the new cabin.

Replacing his hat, Hampton stepped toward her, offering a smile and his hand. "Good to see you."

His comment seemed to melt her reserve, and a full, if bashful, smile blossomed upon her lips. Wordlessly, she tossed him her reins and he led the bay to a new hitching post he had planted.

After he tied the reins, he took her hand, feeling a slight tremor as he helped her from the saddle. She turned from him and quickly opened her saddlebag, removing a bundle of brown paper tied with twine. Charlie offered it to him.

Taking the gift, Hampton untied the string and opened the wad of paper to find a supply of horehound candy. He offered her a piece, which she took, then claimed one for himself. "You're the one who tossed me the candy in jail, weren't you?"

She nodded.

"I was hungry that night."

"I was scared," she replied.

"You should've been, knowing what your father's hands might've done to you."

"Not that," she replied. "I was afraid something might happen to you."

Hampton was touched and felt awkward. No woman had ever seemed to care about his fate. He pointed toward the meager shade of a pecan tree by the dried-up creek, then took her arm and steered her that direction. As he walked, he smiled at the cloud bank still building to the west. In the shade, he released her arm.

Charlie Blunt leaned her back against the tree trunk. Hampton stood opposite her, relishing the beauty of her long black hair, her dark, mysterious eyes, her inviting lips and her breasts, suddenly prominent through her baggy workshirt.

For a moment, Hampton bit his bottom lip, then asked the question he had to have answered. "You know I killed your father, so why did you lie?"

She lowered her head and shut her eyelids for a moment. Hampton feared he had asked the wrong thing until she raised her head. Tears brimmed in her eyes as she started to speak. "The day in the store you gave me candy. No man had ever given me anything out of pure kindness." Tears began to roll down her cheeks.

Hampton felt an urge to take her in his arms and comfort her, but he held back. She had been in too many men's arms, men who had used her to satisfy their lusts. Hampton waited, not wanting her to think he was like the others.

Charlie swiped at her cheeks with the sleeve of her shirt. "Even my own pa used me and Josie like breeding mares. I hated him for what he did and thank you for what you did to him. You gave me a way to get my life back, mine and Josie's. No other man ever did that."

"The other men were wrong." Reaching out, Hampton took her hand. He patted it at first, then lifted it to his lips and kissed it gently. As he did, he heard the faint growl of thunder, but the possibility of rain seemed less important now than did Charlie's tears. "You keep crying, we won't need any rain," he offered.

She laughed through her sobs and pushed herself away from the tree and into Hampton's surprised arms. "Hold me," she said, "just, hold me."

He wrapped his arms around Charlie, pulling her against his chest. Hampton didn't know what to say, so he said nothing — just relished the sweet smells of a woman and the warm fall of her whimpering upon his shoulder. The world was silent except for the sound of her breath and the distant rumble of thunder from the clouds that were boiling up high into the atmosphere.

She remained silently in his arms for a long but pleasant time. When she finally spoke, it was in a whisper. "With Pa dead, Josie and I own the biggest ranch in Brown County, but I need a good man for a foreman. Would you be that man?"

Hampton pondered the invitation for a moment. He wasn't sure he could be comfortable working for a woman he felt this powerfully attracted to. "What does Josie think?"

Charlie shook her head. "Josie won't be staying. She wants a new start, a place where people don't know what happened to her. Me, I want to stay here and prove to people I'm better than my pa and better than what happened to me."

A crack of thunder rattled the ground and the billowing thunderhead blocked out the sun, covering everything with a veil of shade.

Hampton drew her tighter against his chest.

"Would you be my foreman?" she asked, a pleading in her voice.

He nodded slightly. "On one condition."

"What's that?"

"That one day you might consider marrying your foreman."

She sobbed against his chest. "Even though I've been used by many men?"

Hampton nodded as thunder cracked. "I've paid for a woman on occasion, but never one as decent as you."

She pulled away from his chest and kissed him full upon the lips.

Hampton tasted the bitter saltiness of the

tears streaming down her cheeks, but never had he had a sweeter kiss.

Charlie broke away from him. "I would consider marrying my foreman, if my foreman was you."

"I will be your foreman," he said, then kissed her.

They lingered in their embrace for but a moment, then Hampton broke away and sniffed at the air.

As he laughed, Charlie stiffened with worry. "What's wrong? You weren't teasing me, were you?"

"No," Hampton laughed, "you can stop crying. We don't need your tears for irrigation anymore. I can smell rain."

Then they heard the roar of a sudden downpour. They scrambled hand in hand toward the small shed Hampton had built for a barn. Raindrops began to pelt them before they reached cover.

Hampton laughed. "This is what we've been waiting for, praying for. Why are we running?"

Stopping, they threw their arms around each other and let the rain soak them as it pelted the thirsty land.

ABOUT THE AUTHOR

Preston Lewis is the Spur Award-winning author of more than thirty western, juvenile, and historical novels on the Old West as well as numerous articles, short stories, and book reviews on the American frontier.

When he is not writing or researching, Lewis enjoys traveling and photographing historic sites of the Old West and the Civil War.

CPSIA information can be obtained
at www.ICGtesting.com
Printed in the USA
BVHW080158170222
629304BV00008B/8

9 781432 893279